Galaxy voyage

Part 3

The Disc on Shard

LDP Stead

Books by LDP Stead

Galaxy Voyage Part 1
The Dragons of Doom

Galaxy Voyage Part 2
The Sandvipers of Zaak

Galaxy Voyage Part 3
The Disc on Shard

Galaxy Voyage

Part 3

The Disc on Shard

Galaxy Voyage Part 3
The Disc on Shard

ISBN 9781545131923

First Edition Published August 2017

www.galaxy-voyage.co.uk

On-line safety: The website address listed in this book
is correct at the time of print, but please be aware
that online content is subject to change and websites
can contain material unsuitable for children. The
publisher is not responsible for content hosted by third
parties.

For Eleanor, Lucy, Finley, Chloë and Nancy

Chapter 1

The Electra Tower

The kill-bot probe sweeps along through the night, high above the chaotic city below.

It drops down to street level, rushing along above the crowded street filled with creatures of every imaginable shape and size. Tall, purple humanoids, with a single eye in the centre of their foreheads, glance nervously round at a group of furry creatures, who snap at each other with huge mouths full of sharp, vicious teeth. Red, scaly beings in shiny, yellow body suits, locked in a passionate discussion, move to one side without a break in their conversation to make way for a large orange animal with tentacles reaching out from its body on all sides; on its back, on a wide leather saddle, a small hooded figure controls the slow steed's movement with long reins, which stretch to its drooling mouth; occasionally the rider prods the beast with an electrified stick to make it move faster.

The kill-bot probe moves on, humming softly, watching for illegal activity; small lights flash on its sides. On its view-screen the life forms before it appear, each framed briefly in red lines, as the probe scans and identifies: species, weapons, and possible criminal offences.

Suddenly, there is a commotion, a bar fight spills out into the street. Laser pistols are drawn and fired. The probe moves on, it is not concerned with the petty brawls of these poor, lower class citizens. Its job is to protect the rich and powerful in the high-rise towers that stretch up from the smoky streets into the clear night sky.

Rising up the side of one of the towers, the probe flies over the glass roof of a penthouse suite. Inside is a vision of opulence and luxury. Party guests drink, laugh and cavort about a huge swimming pool; scantily-clad dancers drape their arms around the bulbous neck of a giant, green goblin, which is covered with thick, gold necklaces and diamond-encrusted bracelets. The goblin smiles as he is fed living delicacies from a giant platter of squirming food.

The probe moves on. Its sensors detect movement on the tallest tower at the centre of the city. Alerted, it bleeps quietly as it rises up the side of the enormous building which stretches for over a mile into the sky.

Were the probe a person, it would spot a tiny figure, clinging to the side of the metal spire, at the very top of the building; but it is only a machine, and it senses nothing.

Jack keeps perfectly still, and this prevents the kill-bot probe from spotting him as he makes his dangerous ascent up the sheer metal and glass sides of the Central Tower Building. A shield that he has devised blocks the probe's sensors; suction pads, created by 42, hold him in place, he is thousands of metres up, the wind howls around him.

He is almost there. He has climbed the outside of the building from the thousandth floor garden, and now he just has to climb the final fifty feet to the very top. It is a metal spire which tops the building. Zig-zag metal struts form a dangerous, angular ladder for him to climb. He clings on to each piece of cold metal as he pulls himself up, one rung at a time. The icy wind freezes his fingers and tugs at his clothes, trying to dislodge him and throw him to certain death.

He glances down, a mile below are the hazy streets of the city; out of the gloom, giant tower blocks reach up towards him, but even their flat rooftops seem distant, far below. Jack is not afraid of heights, but seeing this view, his stomach lurches, and his vision blurs at the thought of how high he is, and how far he could fall.

Another probe approaches. Jack freezes, keeping absolutely still so that it cannot detect him. It hovers for a moment, then bleeps softly and hums away.

Jack continues to climb again. The tower sways, each step, each rung on the impossible ladder he climbs brings him closer to his goal.

Finally he reaches the very top. Now there is nothing to hold onto but a single, two metre long, metal pole - at the very highest point at the top of the building. On the top of the pole is a flashing light. Holding on with one hand, his feet slipping precariously on a thin metal bar, Jack takes out a knife from a scabbard strapped just above his ankle. He reaches for the light, places the tip of the blade under the rim and strains as he cuts the cover free. It pops off and falls, bouncing down the metal spire, down again past the thousands of windows disappearing into the gloom below.

Jack puts the knife away; then reaches up to the exposed light socket. He can't quite reach, so gripping the pole tightly he pulls himself up and peers into the light socket. There, reflecting and magnifying the light at the top of the tower is a yellow crystal. He has found it! It is the next jewel for the Omicron. Urging his legs to grip the pole with the last of his strength, he reaches in, takes the jewel, thrusts it into a pocket and zips it safely away. Then he lowers himself back to his tiny foothold, turns to face away from the building, takes a deep breath and jumps.

Chapter 2

Memories in the night

Jack fell through the darkness of the night. The huge building on which he had stood moments before, now rushed by next to him, a blur of glass and lights. He extended his arms and stretched out his body.

The flight-suit he wore allowed him to glide; he angled himself away from the building and shot forward towards the other tower blocks below. Falling faster and faster he twisted and turned, the suit making him fly forward as he fell. Between two huge buildings he glided, then onwards aiming towards the edge of town. He smiled; then laughed.

"Yeeeha!" he cried out into the night.

The last few weeks had been intense.

Vendax, the evil ruler of the galaxy and his killer robots had attacked and killed everyone Jack had known at his home in Truno Abbey. All the monks who had brought him up had been killed, including his mentor and teacher, Master Stroud.

Jack had only just escaped with his life on board the small space ship - the Silver FOX, with Lara, a girl with blue skin and long dark hair. She was his best friend.

Before Master Stroud had died, he had given Jack a metal device called the Omicron. Jack had sworn to find the six crystal jewels which fitted holes on the device. Once he had all the jewels, the device would activate a secret weapon which would destroy Vendax and his robot armies. Jack did not yet know how the device worked, but he had voyaged across the galaxy to try and find all the jewels he needed to activate it.

Lara travelled with Jack, equally determined to destroy Vendax, and they had also made other friends along the way- Centurion 42, a kill-bot reprogrammed to help them in their mission; Claws a six-legged, purple cat-like creature; Minnow, a small, white ball of fluff with long, pink arms and legs, and MIM his robot friend.

Together, they had found four of the crystals they needed for the Omicron.

The first they had found in the cave protected by the fearsome dragons of Doom. The next they had managed to snatch from a frozen cavern on the ice world of Sowan, with the teeth of many snow monsters snapping just behind them. To find the third crystal they had battled the vicious Sandvipers of Zaak, losing many new friends in the process, including the beautiful Kendra.

Now Jack had found the fourth jewel for the Omicron. It had been hidden at the very top of the highest tower building in the great city of Electra, at the heart of the empire which Vendax had built.

Here, all people were loyal to Vendax. He had convinced them that he was a wise, powerful leader which they needed. His kill-bots ruled completely and Vendax had absolute control.

This was the place where he rewarded those who had made his rise to power possible. In this place people thought that the kill-bots were peace-keepers, suppressing dangerous rebels, but Jack knew differently. The kill-bots were in fact making unprovoked attacks on innocent, unarmed planets in order to extend Vendax's empire.

Jack's own home planet had been

attacked long ago and his parents killed, leaving him an orphan in the care of kindly monks; now Vendax had destroyed them too and Jack was determined to have his revenge.

Vendax, the giant, white robot with black eyes, and his ambiguous smile, had fooled star-systems that he was a good, caring leader. In truth he was wholly evil.

Jack had sworn to destroy Vendax, and now he had four of the six crystals he needed to activate the Omicron and destroy the evil dictator and his robot armies once and for all.

Jack had lost so much, and there was great sadness in his heart, but he was strong and young, fearless and determined - and right now he was flying through the night, the wind rushing into his face, he was one step nearer his goal, he had good friends, and he was alive!

"Whoo hoo!" He let out another cry of jubilation! He had done it! Another crystal in his possession! He had voyaged across the galaxy, and he would carry on until he had achieved his goal, and Vendax was gone. Nothing was going to stop him!

With a quick flick of his wrist he activated the rip cord on his chest, and a black parachute shot out behind him. The force of the opening chute jerked him upwards; he was now just a few hundred metres from the ground. He smiled again, he had been lucky!

But his luck was about to run out -

All of a sudden, the kill-bot probe which had been patrolling the city earlier reappeared from behind a building. It rushed up to Jack, there was nothing he could do, it had spotted him; it was alerting the kill-bot patrols, they would be after him in moments.

Chapter 3

Kill-biker Attack

A hatch-way opened high up the side of a tall, concrete and glass building. Out shot four kill-bot hover-bikers. The long, sleek vehicles moved with grace and speed; their hover engines humming powerfully, the machinery brand new and of the highest quality. Vendax's army always had the very best equipment, and now the four biker kill-bots angled their machines in pursuit of Jack. They didn't know who he was, but a parachute falling from a tower block looked very suspicious. They had orders to arrest the suspect, and failing that, to kill him.

The lead kill-biker pulled back on his throttle and shot forward; these troops were the elite, their helmets were a different shape to normal kill-bots, they had sharper angles to make them more aero-dynamic, and flashes of red on their white armour to show their special skill and superior rank. At one with their machines, the kill-bikers flashed through the night, eager for the chase, and the kill.

Jack knew the probe must have spotted him. He acted fast. Clicking his heels together, and tapping a control on his forearm, he activated his turbo boosters. Fixed to his back and to the heels of his feet were small, yet powerful rocket packs. With a press of a button he shot forward; the parachute holding him up in the air, and the mini-rockets propelling him forward.

It was a device he had only tried once before - it had not gone well.

It was only for emergencies and was difficult to control. He swung round building after building, all the time gradually falling, but now also being thrust along by the rockets at great speed.

Then the kill-bikers spotted him. They bore down on him and shone bright lights onto his chute.

"Surrender or be destroyed!" came the electronic, amplified voice from the lead bike.

Surrender was not an option. Jack pushed the rockets to turbo and he shot forward, speeding away from the kill-bikers, but he was out of control swinging wildly from one side to another, the rockets on his back and feet leaving a trail of smoke.

"Whoah!" Jack cried out as his body shot forward and the chute dragged behind, the chute folded, he dropped rapidly. The move was unexpected and confused the bikers for a moment, but they soon refocused their pursuit and increased power to their hover-rockets, sweeping in behind him, their fingers ready over their laser-cannon triggers, but Jack's flight path was so chaotic that they couldn't get a clear shot.

Just then, a huge floating screen drifted in front of Jack's way. On the screen was a giant image of Vendax and a news presenter's voice boomed loudly through giant speakers:

"...Lord Vendax has crushed yet another dangerous rebellion with his peace-keeping robots, bringing stability and prosperity to another quadrant of the galaxy..."

The screen had been a surprise. It suddenly blocked Jack's path and he couldn't go round it. He slammed the heel and backpack rockets into reverse in a desperate attempt to slow himself down - but too late! He crashed full force into the floating anti-grav screen; it wobbled and was knocked forward by the force of the collision, smashing into the side of the building behind it.

Jack's chute caught around the top of the screen, and his additional weight now caused it to begin to fall steadily towards the ground.

The kill-bikers were going too fast to stop, so they overshot the floating screen on which Jack hung, but immediately swooped round in a graceful arc to re-focus on their quarry.

Jack was momentarily stunned, but quickly regained his wits, the movement of the floating screen had prevented his impact from being lethal, but now he hung helplessly by his chute down the side of the bright screen which still showed pictures of Vendax and his kill-bots, the news presenter continuing his propaganda speech praising Vendax and proclaiming him to be the 'Glorious Lord of the Galaxy'.

Jack looked below him, then up at the chute above his head. He took out his knife and began to cut himself free. With swift strokes he cut through the strands, and suddenly he dropped. He had timed it just right.

He fell twenty feet, splashing into the pool of a roof garden. The rich family who owned the penthouse suite, and who had been enjoying their luxury garden, screamed as he appeared from nowhere.

The giant screen continued its descent and now wobbling at a crazy angle smashed into the side of another building sending showers of sparks onto the pavement below. Beings of many alien races on the street looked up in alarm.

The kill-bikers watched as the giant screen scraped down the wall, smashing and exploding as it went.

Jack swam quickly to the side of the pool and hauled himself out.

The family cowered in the corner of the roof garden, unused to such a disturbance to their tranquil life of wealth and plenty.

"Please excuse me!" said Jack with an apologetic smile.

"Lara!" he now spoke into a com-link. "I hope you are close by!"

"Right with you!" came Lara's reply.

The kill-bikers, momentarily distracted by the exploding telly-screen, had now spotted Jack again, and were circling round and aiming their bikes towards his position. This was now a priority one case, they would shoot first, and ask questions later - the lead biker took aim, he had Jack in his sights, he squeezed the trigger. Then suddenly, the kill-biker beside him exploded, then a second disappeared in a bright yellow and gold explosion; red laser bolts had blasted the kill-bikers from behind, taking them completely by surprise.

The remaining two bikers split off in different directions to evade the unexpected attack.

Now, between them, a green and black hoverbike flew at full speed; it came to a sudden halt just below where Jack stood on the edge of the building.

The bike hovered still for just a moment and Jack jumped, landing neatly behind the pilot - Lara, dressed in black leather, face concealed with a helmet, but her long dark hair and expert piloting unmistakable, especially to Jack who knew her so well.

Off they shot into the night, at full speed, but the kill-bikers were not going to let them get away that easily. They swept in behind Jack and Lara, blasting with hot, green laser bolts, which shot past them exploding against the sides of buildings, sparks and flames flying off the points of impact.

Lara swung suddenly to the left and then down and to the right, around the side of another building; at full speed she negotiated the maze of buildings with expert skill, skimming low under a bridge, just above street level, then banking sharply and pulling up and over a giant garbage vehicle which made its slow progress through the crowded town. All the time the kill-bikers pursued, but Lara flew with such speed and agility, that they hardly had the chance to a take a shot.

Again, Lara turned sharply, Jack clung on as tightly as he could; only kill-bots could keep up with such daredevil flying - and these kill-bikers were specialist robots, determined to catch or destroy their suspects.

Now, one biker ignited his turbo boost, and pushed his bike to full speed, raining green laser bolts down on Jack and Lara as he shot after them.

They were hit! A blast caught the starboard engine, and sparks and smoke trailed behind them, but Lara gave her vehicle no rest, she used the slowed thrust from the damaged engine, with a boost on the port side thrusters to make a sudden turn to the right.

The manoeuvre caught the kill-biker by surprise, he tried to turn as quickly, but his bike had a much wider turning circle, too late he realised that he'd never make the turn and slammed into the side of a building, exploding in bright red flame; the remains of his bike smashing through the glass and crashing through into the rooms inside.

Lara and Jack's bike was beginning to lose power; black smoke poured from the damaged engine.

The last remaining kill-biker could see that they were in trouble; he was more determined than ever to destroy them. He tucked his head down, lined Jack and Lara up in his sights and accelerated.

Lara accelerated too, hitting the turbo button, knowing that this might cause the hover-vehicle to explode, but also knowing it was their only chance of escape.

"Are you ready, 42?" cried Lara.

"I am ready," came 42's calm reply.

Jack and Lara shot over a dark hole in the ground. As soon as they had passed it, the Silver FOX rose from the hole, and now faced the kill-biker head on. The biker tried to slow down and turn, but he was too late, the Silver FOX fired with all weapons and the kill-biker disappeared in a bright, dazzling explosion; his high-tech bike shredded into thousands of metallic fragments which span off in all directions.

Claws at the weapon controls of the Silver FOX celebrated with a long feline roar; the little ball of white fluff which was Minnow, jumped up and down with excitement on the control panel, waving his little pink arms.

"Minnow! Minnow!" he cried in delight that Jack and Lara were safe.

42, as calm as ever in the pilot seat, brought the Silver FOX round until it hovered just above where Jack and Lara now disembarked from the burning hover-bike.

They jumped up onto the open

service-ramp and climbed inside; the Silver FOX sped away from the huge city; behind it their speeder bike exploded.

With Jack, Lara and the fourth crystal now safely on board, the Silver FOX arced round and aimed upwards away from the planet towards the edge of the atmosphere; the darkness of space filled the view screen, they were in the clear.

"Making the fold-jump," said Lara.

The space-fold engines roared and the Silver FOX sped away faster than light.

"Kendra – we're on our way," said Jack.

Chapter 4

Rescue

The Silver FOX streaked across the blue sky high above planet Zaak. Below, the white hot sands of the unending desert spread out in all directions.

"This is where Kendra's base was," said Lara.

"Let's hope that she made it," replied Jack, his face serious.

"I hope that Vendax is kept busy with our last attack, at least for a while," said Lara.

"Yes," agreed Jack, "although I'm

worried he might already be after us."

"They might still be here," added 42 ominously.

The crew of the Silver FOX all peered through the view-screen, desperate to see something, some sign of life, some indication that Kendra and her friends had escaped the kill-bot ambush and the attack of the sandvipers.

Had Kendra escaped the kill-bots and managed to find somewhere to hide out in the caves, or had the kill-bots caught up with her? None of them knew what they would find.

"Scanners are on maximum," reported Lara.

"Don't forget that the kill-bots would use the same scanners as ours, and Kendra wouldn't want them to find her. If she is trying to hide, she might be blocking our signal," said Jack.

"How are we going to find them then?" asked Lara.

"Take us down - can you find their base? Maybe they left us a clue," said Jack. "If she's alive, she would know that we would come back for her."

Lara glanced at Jack, but he didn't notice her look; he was staring out of the view-screen, still looking for any sign of Kendra.

Suddenly the intercom crackled to life:

"Well - you certainly took your time didn't you!" Kendra's voice over the radio was unmistakable.

"Kendra!" cried Jack. "You're alive! Thank goodness!"

"It would take more than a few kill-bots to finish us," laughed Kendra.

"Where are you?" asked Jack.

"I'm sending the co-ordinates," replied Kendra.

Soon, the Silver FOX had landed, and Kendra and her people flooded out around the ship, pleased to be out of their hiding place in caves deep below a rocky outcrop. All about them buzzed the little robot MIMs bleeping and buzzing in delight.

Laughing and smiling, Kendra ran towards Jack as he appeared on the service-ramp, she wrapped her arms around him and kissed him on one cheek, then the other, over and over.

"I knew you would make it back!" she said. "Claws!" she exclaimed and hugged the cat, who hugged back with all four arms.

Lara, as always was a little overwhelmed by Kendra, but she too soon found herself being welcomed with hugs and kisses too.

Kendra was full of life and energy, but it was clear that she and her people had not found things easy since they had helped find the Omicron jewel.

They were tough and resourceful, but the battle against the sandvipers had been hard, and so had the escape from the kill-bots; without the MIMs to create all the things they needed they would never have survived, and now all they wanted was to be finally off this planet.

"Claws, will you send the signal to the transport?" asked Jack.

Claws nodded and spoke into a communicator in his cat-language.

It was not long before the large Clorn-Arduan transport landed on the sands, and Kendra's people gratefully climbed aboard. The cat-people had been most impressed by the stories of Kendra's survival in the desert and had promised to care for her and her people on Duatha.

It was not long before Kendra's people were all on board and ready to depart. It was a huge relief to have found Kendra safe, but now it seemed no time at all before it was time to say goodbye again.

Kendra stood by the service-ramp of the transport ship and spoke to Jack, Lara, 42, Claws and Minnow.

"Thank you for coming back for me," Kendra said. "You had better not stay here long - if Vendax has a trace on your ship, it won't take him long to find you."

"Yes, we have to go," said Jack sadly. "Thank you for your help. Without you and your people, we would not have the red crystal; and our mission to destroy Vendax would have already failed. We are forever grateful. We will see you all on Duatha soon."

"Without you, we could have been marooned here forever," replied Kendra. "It was an honour to help you in your quest. I would dearly love to come and help you to look for the last of the crystal jewels, but my place is with my people, they need me."

"We understand," said Jack. "You have done more than enough already."

Kendra embraced them each in turn, then she turned and walked up the ramp of the transport, she waved and the hatch closed.

The Clorn-Arduan transport ship lifted off, taking Kendra and her people to safety. The others boarded the Silver FOX. Their hearts felt lighter knowing that Kendra was safe; they knew that they would see her again, but now it was time to find the next crystal. The Silver FOX lifted off and shot up into the sky.

Chapter 5

Lanza

The fold-tunnel sped by in a blur past the view-screen as the Silver FOX rushed towards its next destination far across the galaxy.

Jack, Lara, Claws, 42 and Minnow sat round the table at the centre of the little ship. In front of them was the Omicron. They now had four of the six crystal jewels that would activate it and destroy Vendax; they still didn't know how it worked, but Jack had absolute faith in his mentor, Master Stroud, who had given him the Omicron as he had died when Vendax had attacked Truno Abbey.

"So, tell me more about this next planet we are due to visit," said Jack.

"It is called 'Lanza' and it is a planet that is entirely covered with water; an ocean planet," replied Lara.

"No land at all?" asked Jack.

"No land that shows up on the long range scan or the computer records," frowned Lara.

"How will we find a jewel if it's all just water?" asked Jack.

Claws and Minnow looked at each other and shrugged.

"Perhaps it is somewhere on the water, or even underwater?" ventured 42 in his deep robotic voice.

"Maybe," said Jack, "I guess that the only way to find out is to get there and see what we find."

Twelve hours later the crew of the Silver FOX peered through the view-screen at the huge planet that appeared glowing before them in the blackness of space; it was completely blue.

"All water," mused Jack. "I didn't know there were planets like this."

"Me neither; looks like finding the crystal will not be easy," said Lara. "Here we go again!"

Claws let out a slight growl, a look of concern on his face at the thought of the difficulty of the task they faced and the unknown dangers ahead.

The Omicron bleeped on the console indicating that the next jewel was on the planet below. Lara tapped the keyboard of the navi-computer, and they started their approach.

As they entered the atmosphere, the Silver FOX juddered as the shields fended off the intense heat created by the friction of the small craft hitting the air around the planet.

Then their descent eased into a slow glide, and before them was the deep blue of continuous ocean that spread as far as the eye could see. The water was dark and deep, and as the wind blew across the surface, white crests appeared on the top of the waves.

The Omicron bleeped, showing the direction they should follow. Then, on the horizon, something caught Jack's eye. It was some sort of structure, built on surface of the water.

"What's that over there?" he asked.

The others all followed his gaze and spotted the structure. As they approached they could see that it was really quite large; it was some sort of floating town built on the ocean.

As the Silver FOX approached, the companions could see that the large town was constructed out of the floating hulls of numerous vehicles; some ocean-going ships, some space vehicles, all rusted and broken, but still able to float. In the very centre, was a large tanker, to which all the other vessels were bound. The whole place seemed deserted.

"Shall we take a look?" said Jack. "There might be things here we can use."

"I'm not sure," replied Lara. "There is something ominous about this place. It makes me nervous."

"We do need more material for the matter-energy converter," said 42. "Sensors show that there is some appropriate material in the centre of the structure; it would keep our engines fuelled for quite some time."

"We may not get another chance like this to re-fuel," said Jack," besides, it looks interesting." He peered inquisitively at the ramshackle structure with its precarious walkways and mismatched components all lashed randomly together.

"Well, I suppose it might be better to get what we need here, rather than finding it in a place crawling with kill-bots," replied Lara, "but let's make it quick; remember that it won't take long for Vendax to get a trace on our position. We need to get the crystal from this planet and get away fast."

"Ok," said Jack. "We'll be quick."

Lara brought the Silver FOX to hover next to the ocean town and then gradually lowered the ship into the waves. The spaceship was air-tight and designed to float on water just as well as to fly through the vacuum of space.

The companions climbed out of the upper hatch of the Silver FOX and stood on top of the little ship as it bobbed gently on the waves. Claws jumped onto the edge of the floating city and threw a rope to Jack who secured the Silver FOX.

Lara and Minnow stayed with the ship whilst the others made their way to the centre of the floating construction.

Up close, they could see the inventiveness of the people who had built this floating town. It was made of all manner of salvaged parts, lashed together with ropes, wire and a kind of strong black seaweed. Another type of weed had been used as a sort of resin to seal holes and bond different elements of the structure firmly together. The place certainly had an eerie feel; it was completely silent except the lapping of the waves beneath them.

"I wonder what happened to every-body?" said Jack.

"Look!" said 42, "that cooking pot on the table..."

"Yes?" said Jack.

 "It's still hot!" said 42.

"Still hot? Someone must be here!" exclaimed Jack.

Suddenly, there was movement all around them; the very surface of the floating town seemed to come alive as creatures emerged from hiding places all about them.

They were taken completely by surprise, and before they could reach for their weapons, they found themselves face-to-face with spears and arrows from every direction. Then firm hands seized them, and their weapons were quickly whisked away.

The citizens of the floating city now surrounded them, and the once silent ocean dwelling was now a hubbub of noise and activity. The people themselves were about the size of humans, but had scaly green and white striped skin and webbed hands and feet, they breathed as humans did, but also had gills behind their ears. Some swam in the sea and were clearly as agile in the water as they were on the land. They had yellow eyes with vertical slits as pupils, and in their mouths were an array of viciously sharp, pointed teeth.

The sea-creatures were not technologically advanced, but had a highly-skilled primitive intelligence. They communicated with clicking, whirring noises and were all very excited about capturing the Silver FOX and its crew.

The most worrying thing was the variety of weapons the creatures carried; as well as spears and arrows, they brandished dangerous looking knives and blades, some made from scrap material they had salvaged, and others from the teeth of sea animals. All the weapons looked like they would cause a great deal of damage and pain if they were used.

Jack, Claws and 42 were bound with seaweed rope. 42 could easily have escaped his bonds, but did not dare take the risk, as his companions were being threatened with the nasty looking weapons; he could not hope to save them before they were seriously injured. Instead the three of them bided their time, waiting for a chance to escape, and hoping that Lara might see what had happened and come to their rescue.

Suddenly, drums started all around them and the sea-creatures began wailing and hooting, their shrill voices kicking up a great noise as the three companions were pushed and shoved towards the large tanker at the centre of the floating town.

As they approached, an unwelcome sight met their eyes. The creatures had captured Lara. She was bound by seaweed rope and was standing at knife point at the highest point on the tanker. Above her was a pulley and she was tied to a rope which then ran up and over the pulley; it looked as if the sea-creatures meant to lower her with the rope into the body of the tanker.

Jack, Claws and 42 looked up as they were pushed to where Lara stood. This was not good news. They had all hoped Lara might come to their rescue, but it seemed that she was in a worse position than they were. The drumming and wailing intensified and a sea-creature with an elaborate headdress and cloak, with piercings all over his face and body, appeared in front of Lara. The other sea-creatures clearly feared and respected this leader; they bowed their heads and waved their arms towards him as he approached.

Jack could see that Lara was scared, but was doing her best to put on a brave face. The sea-creature in the headdress approached and moved his face close to hers; she tried to turn her head away, but another creature held her, so that she had to face this leader. He was chanting, his sharp teeth chattering, as he came close, Lara could smell fish and salt water on his breath; he reached out with both hands and placed a necklace of shells around her neck.

By now Jack, Claws and 42 had reached the platform where Lara was held captive. From here they could see that she had been placed on a precarious ledge of rusty metal, and that below her was a long drop to the bottom of the tanker. To their horror they saw that the floor was covered in bones, some were the skeletons of fish, but many were the unmistakable skeletons and skulls of human beings. Around their necks were the same shell necklaces which Lara now wore.

The drumming and chanting reached a new peak, and suddenly Lara was hoisted up in the air; the bindings tightening painfully. She was swung out and over the long drop to the bottom of the hollow tanker, and then was lowered roughly down. Finally, her feet bumped against the floor. She cast a frightened look below her as her feet dislodged a pile of white bones.

At the other end of the tanker several creatures grasped another seaweed rope and began to pull. A hush fell over the crowd, and some of the other sea-creatures blew into shells making a long discordant sound.

As the creatures pulled at the rope, a large metal door was being hauled slowly upwards, behind it was darkness. Lara stared inside; it seemed that something horrific dwelt in the dark interior of the ship, and it was now being let loose on her.

She struggled to try and free herself, but was held tight by the sea-weed rope.

Then she heard a sound. The crowd of sea-creatures heard it too, and an excited hush fell over them. It was a clicking sound, and a tap, tap, tap of many feet on the metal hull of the tanker.

Jack, Lara and 42 all peered down trying to see what would emerge from the black hole.

Again the sounds came, louder this time, and then there was a sharp – 'snap, snap'. Lara was terrified, unable to escape, she saw a shadow move in the darkness behind the doorway, and then it emerged.

A giant crab edged its way out into

the sunlight. Its body was about three metres in diameter, its legs made it twice that size, they clicked on the metal of the boat as it moved; shuffling through broken bones, its small, beady eyes, which stuck out on long stalks, peered at Lara. It snapped its pincers, as it approached hungrily. It scuttled towards her; then stopped, assessing its surroundings, glancing up at the excited crowd of sea-creatures who watched with morbid excitement from above. The crab's body was green with black dappled spots and the tips of its legs and pincers were a threatening red. It was surprisingly agile for its size; it scuttled forward again, closer to Lara, who struggled helplessly against the ropes that held her.

Jack and Claws pushed forward and were met by razor-sharp weapons inches from their faces.

42 stood ready, silent, waiting for the right moment to make his move, but

no solutions presented themselves. It seemed likely that no matter what he did, some or all of his companions might die.

Chapter 6

King Thraad

The giant crab moved closer towards Lara. She could see its mouth, filled with rows of sharp, little teeth, opening and closing; tasting the air, ready to feed.

Suddenly, its huge pincers snapped quickly open and closed. Lara jumped; she could see they were powerful enough to cut her in two with one swift movement. She tried to edge away, but the rope was already pulled taught, and she could not escape, struggling only made her swing back even closer towards the approaching giant crustacean.

Jack, Claws and 42 watched in horror. The crab suddenly scuttled forwards and raised its pincers ready to make the killer strike.

That was it, 42 made his move; breaking free of his bonds, he struck out at the sea-creatures who were pointing weapons at Jack and Claws, sweeping them aside with his strong metal arms. Jack and Claws had been ready, and kicked out with their legs, knocking more sea-creatures out of the way. It was a desperate move, it worked for a moment, but then more of the creatures swarmed towards them with weapons raised, angry that they had been attacked and that their entertainment had been disturbed.

Jack felt something tugging at the ropes which bound him, and looking down he saw that it was Minnow.

"Minnow! Minnow!" chirped the little ball of fluff as he cut through Jack's ropes; then MIM appeared and floated over to Claws to free him too.

42 barred the way to protect Jack and Claws; he used his huge metal body as a shield to deflect the spears and knives which the sea-creatures thrust forward.

All of sudden, a metal, laser-tipped spear flew through the air and pierced the raised pincer of the giant crab. The huge crustacean recoiled in pain, anger and surprise and backed away from Lara.

A great commotion erupted among the sea-creatures - someone else was attacking them!

Leaping athletically, brandishing cutlasses and laser-pistols, were bearded sailors, large ear-rings in their ears, rings on their fingers, long braided hair, ragged clothes and muscular, tattooed bodies. They were a tough bunch.

One sailor hurled himself into the air, flying into the sea-creatures guarding Lara's rope. They fell helplessly over the side into the sea.

Then several other sailors seized the rope and jumped into the crab pit. This launched Lara into the air, out of the reach of the giant crab. The huge animal had snapped off the end of the spear which had struck its pincer, and now, angered and hungry, it waved its pincers aggressively at the sailors, but they held it at bay by stabbing at it with their swords.

As Lara swung upwards, her breath was momentarily taken away in surprise, but she soon understood what was happening and stared down at the men who had bravely used their own weight to lift her away from danger, but she still hung precariously over the pit. Suddenly, she was seized by strong arms which wrapped around her.

"Hold tight, don't worry, I've got you." said the deep voice of her rescuer, who had swung dangerously out over the crab pit, caught her expertly on the back swing, and now whisked her through the air to the safety of the platform at the top of the tanker.

Lara's face pressed against the tattooed chest of the sailor, and she could smell his musky, salty scent and the strength of his muscles tightening as he held her and landed her gently on the platform.

She looked up at him, he was young and handsome, yet his face showed that he was wise and experienced for his years. He smiled widely with a charming, infectious grin producing dimples in his lightly-bearded cheeks. His blue eyes sparkled with good humour and they never left Lara's face despite the dangerous battle which raged about them.

A sea-creature suddenly lunged at

them, brandishing a sharp knife; without taking his eyes off Lara the sailor punched the creature straight on the nose and it fell off the tanker and into the sea.

The sailor's grin widened again.

"Terribly sorry about that!" he said gallantly. Then he produced a sharp knife, and with a swift movement cut Lara's rope. She gasped in surprise as she was suddenly set free by the dangerous looking blade.

"Captain Flash, at you service!" proclaimed the sailor, removing his tricorn hat and sweeping low in an elaborate bow.

"And you," Flash continued. "You are beautiful! I have never seen such beauty in all my days on the sea and in the sky! May I have the honour of knowing you name?"

 Lara blushed, she was not used to

being talked to like this and it made her a little uncomfortable, but the sailor was so charming and kind, not to mention handsome.

"I'm Lara," she replied. Her voice wobbled slightly as she spoke, and she was annoyed with herself for not sounding more confident.

"Lara! Lara! - it is an honour and a pleasure to meet you, Lara!"

Jack, Claws, 42 and Minnow appeared on the platform to see Captain Flash holding Lara's hand, gazing into her eyes; his arm around her shoulders.

"Lara! You are truly beautiful! A gift from the Gods! What a blessed day this is, that such beauty should come into my life!" continued Flash oblivious to everything going on around him.

"What's he talking to her like that for?" said Jack frowning.

"Jack!" called Lara as she saw the others approaching.

Captain Flash jumped to his feet and smiled.

"Ah! your companions, Lara! I have watched them fight most honourably this day!"

Just then a group of sea-creatures appeared at the other side of the platform. Leading them was the same creature that had placed the shell necklace on Lara; he still wore his dramatic headdress, and he gnashed his teeth threateningly as he approached.

The sea-creatures behind him were rallied by his attack and gathered to watch him fight. He was armed with a jagged sword in each hand, and his face was menacing and dangerous as he moved towards Captain Flash and Lara; he clearly meant to re-take her and carry out the sacrifice he had started.

Captain Flash turned and faced the king of the sea-creatures, unafraid, a smile on his face as he drew his cutlass from its scabbard. He barred the way to Lara.

"So! King Thraad! You are still ruling your good people with your evil ways! I think that today is the day your rule is over! No more sacrifices Thraad!" said Flash as he and the sea-creature circled each other.

Lara ran to Jack, Claws and the others who stood at one side of the tanker platform with a group of sailors who had also gathered to watch the leaders fight. Across the floating town the other fighting had stopped, now all eyes were on this final battle.

Thraad the king of the sea-creatures spat out some guttural sounds and thrust forward, swinging his swords wildly and powerfully at Flash.

"Language! Language!" said Flash, tutting in mock disproval as if talking to a small child, completely unconcerned by Thraad's attack which he parried aside easily with several skillful flicks of his sword.

"Your people lived happily and peacefully until you and your thugs came along and took over, luring ships into your traps! Terrorising your own people! Living sacrifices made to imaginary gods! Really - it's just not nice!" continued Flash.

Again Thraad attacked, goaded by Flash's words. This time his attack was prolonged, and he brought his weapons round in great swirling loops which Flash just managed to duck and avoid, but which would have finished a less skilled fighter. The two ended up with swords locked, and then with a great shove, Jack pushed them apart again.

Jack quickly put the smile back on his

face.

"Well, Thraad! Looks like you've been practising! New moves, eh? Well -they might work on your women and children, but you'll have to do better than that if you want to fight me! It's about time you picked on someone your own size!"

Again, Thraad attacked in a whirl of flashing, razor-sharp blades, snarling, spinning and kicking. Despite Flash's nonchalant words and apparent relaxed confidence, Thraad was clearly a fearsome opponent. The sailors and sea-creatures watched in gripped silence.

Flash and Thraad moved this way and that around the platform, thrusting and parrying with their swords. Thraad's attacks were vicious and brutal, Flash's elegant and skillful.

In a sudden move, Thraad rolled at Flash and knocked him from his feet,

Thraad hurled himself at Flash and landed on top of him; their swords trapped between their bodies, Thraad leaned his head towards Flash's throat, gnashing his pointed teeth, almost reaching him, pushing with great strength, to try and kill Flash with a bite to the jugular vein.

It took all of Flash's strength to hold Thraad at bay. The sailors watching had their hands on their swords ready to intervene, but they should have known their leader better. With a quick move, Flash head-butted Thraad, and threw him to one side, then leapt to his feet, picking up his sword as he moved. He was back on his feet, and ready again.

"Now, that was just plain nasty!" said Flash, brushing his shirt where Thraad's green drool had fallen as he had tried to bite him; still deliberately maintaining his relaxed, conversational style despite the dangers of the battle.

Thraad on the other hand was clearly furious, and muttering nasty sea-creature oaths, he hurled himself at Flash again.

This time, Flash was ready for him. Twisting to one side he flicked away one of Thraad's swords. Then ducking, spinning and with an upward thrust of his cutlass, he knocked the sword out of the sea-creature king's other hand. Then Flash stuck his booted leg behind Thraad, and the creature was so off-balance, all it took was a gentle shove on his shoulders to knock the scaled tyrant down and onto his back. Flash placed his sword at Thraad's throat.

"It's over, Thraad!" Flash now spoke seriously. "Give it up. Leave your people and renounce your leadership."

Jack, Lara, Claws, 42 and Minnow had watched in amazement at the skill with which Flash had fought. Now they and the other sailors readied themselves in case the other sea-creatures should attack - but they did not.

It seemed that Flash was right and perhaps the sea-creatures were not as loyal to their leader as they had seemed.

All eyes were on Flash and the fallen king. Thraad looked angry, but then he bowed his head in defeat. Flash slowly took his sword from Thraad's throat.

"Let it be known among all your people that Thraad is no longer king," pronounced Flash. "There will be no more terror, and no more sacrifices. You are free again to be the peaceful people you once were."

As Flash spoke, the sea-creatures dropped their weapons and some began to smile and cheer. Clearly Thraad had not been a popular leader, and they were glad to see him go.

Yet even as everyone began to relax, suddenly, Thraad was on his feet, and attacked Flash again. Pulling a small, vicious, jagged blade from somewhere hidden in his robes, he hurled himself at Flash whose back was turned.

Flash reacted quickly; he caught Thraad's shoulders, turned to one side, and using the force of Thraad's own attack, propelled him up and over the railing around the platform.

Everyone watched as the evil king fell down into the giant crab pit. In this pit the tyrant had put many people to death. He had meant Lara to die here, but instead, it was he who now lay among the bones, staring terrified into the dark doorway at the end of the tanker.

The giant crab came; it scuttled forward, quickly towered above Thraad and raised its pincers. Thraad gave a high-pitched scream of terror.

The pincers moved swiftly and Thraad met his end. The crab scuttled back into the darkness to eat its meal; one half of King Thraad in each of its giant pincers.

"Well," said Flash, grimacing with distaste. "That's the end of him!"

Chapter 7

The Wave Star

At the death of their leader, the remaining sea-creatures dropped their weapons and backed away, many jumping into the sea, and some bowing respectfully to Captain Flash before they turned and disappeared.

"They really are kindly people." explained Flash to Jack and the others. "Their race is called the 'Webben'. They have lived for thousands of years on this planet; in and on the sea, living a simple peaceful life; until Thraad came along with a gang of his thugs and enslaved them all. If they disagreed with him they were fed to the giant crab beastie. I'm afraid you were lured here by their trap - the promise of free matter-energy conversion material for your engines - you are not the first ship they have caught - but enough history for now! Welcome to Lanza! Planet of water! I am Captain Flash, and these are the men and women who choose to sail with me!"

The sailors all around them nodded in greeting, and then Jack stepped forward.

"I am Jack," he said, "and Lara you have met."

"Yes indeed - the beautiful Lara!" interrupted Flash, looking longingly at Lara, and smiling.

Lara looked uncomfortable, and to her embarrassment, blushed slightly, her blue skin turning purple around her cheeks.

Jack then introduced, Claws, 42,

Minnow and MIM to the sailors.

"You certainly are an unusual crew! You have fought valiantly with us today, and you are most welcome. I have many questions, but here is not the place. I invite you all to dine aboard my vessel, where we can talk in comfort."

The crew of the Sliver FOX accepted his invitation gratefully, and followed Flash and the other sailors back to where they had boarded the floating town. There was the Sliver FOX, tied up where they had left it, but there was no sign of any other vessel.

Flash smiled when he saw their expressions.

"I suppose you are wondering where my ship is moored?" he asked with a broad smile. "Allow me to present my humble vessel - 'The Wave Star'."

With that, Flash pointed a small

device, which he held in his hand, at the empty waves just behind the Silver FOX, and pressed a button.

Something began to appear on the sea before them. The light rippled and shimmered over it, and as if by magic, a magnificent ship appeared on the sea, where moments before there had been nothing at all.

"Wow!" said Jack. "You must have some sort of cloaking-device. I've never seen one before."

Flash smiled, clearly delighted with his surprise, and obviously very proud of his vessel. It was quite a ship. Although floating on the waves at the moment, it was a space vessel just like the Silver FOX, but three times the size, the hull was sleek, streamlined and angular, and it sparkled, metallic gold in the bright sunshine.

"Please come on board!" offered Flash. He spoke to all the companions, but his eyes were on Lara and this invite he seemed to offer directly to her. He extended his arm and before she had time to think, her arm was linked in his, and she was walking along by his side.

Jack watched as Flash and Lara walked together up the boarding-ramp of the Wave Star. He felt annoyed, Flash had certainly saved them, and seemed a good person, but he didn't like the way he spoke to Lara; she wasn't the sort of person who liked being flattered, yet here she was arm-in-arm with him. He felt a knot in his stomach.

Flash strode up the boarding-ramp, confident and cheerful, he held Lara's arm gently, but she could feel the strength of his body next to hers.

Again she felt herself blushing slightly. Why had she taken his arm? She should be with the others - with her friends, with Jack. Yet Flash made it so easy, he swept her up to his ship, considerate and attentive in every way. She didn't feel she could just go back to the others, Flash had just saved her life, and Lara had never been given so much attention before, let alone by someone so handsome.

She glanced back and for a moment caught Jack's eye; she smiled, he smiled back; then looked awkwardly away.

"Come on board!" said Flash, taking her hand and supporting her as she entered the golden vessel.

The others followed, and soon they were all aboard. Flash led them to a large room, at its centre a dining table.

"Please bring us food and drink!" He energetically gave the order to some of his sailors.

 Soon they were all seated around the

table with cold fruit juices and a wide variety of delicious foods to suit all tastes laid out before them.

The room was spacious and luxurious with highly polished surfaces; yet it was made homely and welcoming with large, soft cushions, decorative hangings, and interesting artefacts from across the galaxy displayed on illuminated shelves. Where ever you looked there was something to catch your eye, and it seemed that behind each item was a different story of adventure and discovery waiting to be told. Flash and his crew had obviously travelled far, and been on many adventures.

"This was my father's ship," explained Flash. "Our family travelled the stars; my parents were archaeologists, seeking artefacts from ancient races across the galaxy. There was no traditional education for me. My parents and I travelled, they taught me everything I needed to know as we went; and I learned from the different races and tribes that we encountered. What better life could a child want? Freedom, adventure, travelling the stars, meeting every imaginable type of person, seeing, hearing, feeling the most incredible things!"

Lara looked around at the luxurious interior, Flash's enthusiasm for adventure and his zest for life was infectious.

"I share my parents' fascination with ancient civilizations," continued Flash. "Most people presume that technology was less advanced in the past; but this is not so. We have discovered unbelievable wonders, evidence of people living thousands of years ago who were far more advanced than we are now. Just one example is the cloaking-device you saw me use on this ship; that is not new technology, but a relic of the ancients. But anyway; enough about me, what is it that brings you here?" asked Flash.

Jack glanced at Lara. Flash seemed friendly and he had helped them, but should they risk telling him about their quest? Jack decided not to tell him everything yet.

"We have come here in search of a rare crystal jewel," Jack explained. "It is not valuable in itself, but it is of great importance to my family." Jack showed Flash the Omicron. "We have this device which will lead us to it."

Flash looked at the Omicron.
"May I see?" he asked.

Jack handed the device to him and Flash looked at it intently, turning it over; looking at the map on the back and running his finger over the markings.

"Interesting," said Flash. "Well, I love an adventure, and finding artefacts is what I do. If you will accept our help, my crew and I are at your disposal. Do these arrows point to the object you seek?"

Jack nodded.

"Excellent," continued Flash with a smile. "Shall we a start straight away?"

Jack and Lara smiled in agreement. "Thank you, Flash, we would appreciate your help!"

Chapter 8

The Temple

The Wave Star and the Silver FOX made ready to set off in search of the fifth Omicron crystal. Captain Flash issued orders to his crew who leapt to their tasks with skill and efficiency to make ready to get under way.

"I would be honoured if you would sail with me aboard the Wave Star," said Flash to Lara.

"I think it is best if I'm at the controls of the Silver FOX," replied Lara politely, "but thank you." She turned to join the others as they boarded their ship.

Captain Flash, as confident as ever, waved his hand in gracious acceptance of her decision - "Another time then perhaps, Lara."

Jack found a slight smile creeping over his face. He was pleased Lara was coming with them instead of Flash.

Soon they were away, skimming the waves, the Silver FOX in the lead and the Wave Star just behind.

They had used the navi-com to plot a course to where the crystal lay and the Omicron bleeped steadily showing that they were on target.

Jack and Lara knew they must be quick; the battle with the Webben had cost them valuable time. Vendax would soon be on to them. They had to get the crystal and get away fast before his terror-naughts found them again. Fortunately it was not far and they soon reached the location where the Omicron indicated the crystal could be found.

"Is this it?" asked Jack.

"This is the spot," replied Lara.

"Unfortunately, there's nothing here," frowned Jack.

They all peered at the water below the ship.

"It looks like 42 was right. The crystal must be under the surface of the ocean," said Lara.

They had hoped that the crystal might be on a small island or on a vessel floating on the sea; that would have been much easier, but they were prepared for this too.

The Silver FOX and the Wave Star settled onto the surface of the water. In the hull of the Wave Star a panel opened and a ramp extended to the sea. A small deep-sea vehicle appeared and steadily made its way down into the ocean. The vehicle was oval shaped and had two extendable robotic arms. The panels at the front and along the sides were transparent so the crew could see underwater. At its helm was Captain Flash.

The mini-sub entered the water and made its way towards the Sliver FOX where Jack and Lara climbed aboard. 42, Claws and Minnow watched from the cockpit of the Silver FOX. MIM hovered over the deep-sea vehicle, and when its crew was safely on board he closed the hatch and they secured it from the inside.

MIM hovered back to the open hatch way of the Silver FOX, entered and landed next to Minnow, who put his little pink arm around his robot friend. They both peered anxiously out at the mini-sub as it slowly disappeared beneath the waves.

Inside the sub, Flash, Lara and Jack sat on comfortable, padded plastic seats, Flash at the controls at the front, and Jack and Lara on the seat behind.

"We use this vehicle for exploring submerged ruins," said Flash. "We can dive up to 1000 feet, after that the pressure will be dangerous. Our sonar reading shows that there is a structure of some kind not far below the surface. My parents often explored this planet, it was once inhabited by a great civilisation, it had much land and many cities and towns, but there was a planet wide catastrophe, a change in the planet's orbit brought the poles closer to the sun and the ice caps melted, the sea level rose and the population had to be quickly evacuated."

The mini-sub went deeper and deeper under the waves. The light from the surface gradually faded.

"Activating lights," said Flash.
With the flick of several switches,
powerful spotlights shone out from the
deep-sea vehicle and Jack and Lara
could see clearly into the water
around them.

Fish darted by through the bubbles
from their craft, tiny plankton
shimmered in the spot lights, they
moved steadily forward, the hull
making slight creaking sounds as they
went deeper and the water pressure
around them increased.

"Look there!" said Lara.

They all looked forward; gradually
appearing from the distant gloom
was the outline of a ruined building.

It looked like it had once been some
sort of temple on the top of a
mountain, and now it stuck out on its
own from the bottom of the sea.
Areas had crumbled, but most of the
building was intact, although covered

in long grass-like seaweed.

Flash moved the sub closer. The Omicron bleeped, its arrow direction finders clearly showing that the next jewel was somewhere in the temple.

"Can we take the sub in?" asked Jack.

"It doesn't look like the entrance is big enough," replied Flash, "and it could be dangerous; the vibrations from the engines might bring the whole structure down. We'll have to go in ourselves."

Jack and Lara nodded. The three of them prepared, pulling their diving masks on and attaching their mini-aqua lungs; they sat ready for the compartment to flood.

Flash gave a thumbs-up sign, Lara and Jack returned the signal. They were ready. Flash flicked several switches and now the compartment began to flood. The water was cold and despite the diving equipment Lara felt a surge of panic. Flash took her arm and looked intently into her the eyes, nodding with reassurance. She felt herself calming down.

The water gushed into the little sub and now it bubbled up and over their heads. They breathed through the aqualungs. The pressure was equalised, Flash lifted the canopy; they drifted out. Securing the mini-sub with a nylon rope to the side of the underwater temple, they made their way in.

There was a hole where part of the structure had collapsed long ago; it was covered in weeds and completely dark inside. The three of them made their way inside, shining underwater torches as they went.

Fish darted past them, startled by the lights and the bubbles drifting up from their breathing apparatus. They made their way in deeper.

Suddenly, as Flash moved forward, there was a great gush of bubbles and a creature rushed past. Flash flinched backwards and the others gasped, their heartbeats racing; but it was only an eel, disturbed from its hiding place. Its long, sleek green body slipped passed them.

"Are you OK?" asked Flash through their intercom.

"Yes, I'm fine," said Lara," - just a shock that's all."

Flash nodded in reassurance.
"Ok, which way now?" he said, indicating the Omicron which Lara held in a waterproof container.

"Over there," said Lara, pointing down a long passage way.

They continued through the dark water, their torches illuminating the walls of the ancient temple which was decorated with carvings and mosaics of great detail and intricacy. Finally, they came to a doorway; the wooden door itself had long since rotted away leaving a wide opening into a large central chamber.

The three of them swam in, their torches shining onto tall statues of creatures with the bodies of humans and the heads of animals. Flash shone his torch over one of the statues, clearly fascinated.

"This is quite a find. I'm going to come back here once all this is over and take a closer look!" he said.

Then through the gloom they saw two glowing purple eyes starring directly at them. Lara gasped and grabbed Jack's arm, Flash swam on, beckoning them to follow.

Lara and Jack hesitantly followed, yet as they approached, they understood what they had seen. At the centre of the chamber was a huge statue of a goddess, it was magnificent, even after all these years; it was her eyes which were glowing. Jack and Lara had seen this sort of glowing light before. The other Omicron crystals had also glowed in a similar way. They knew the crystal jewel must be inside the head, its light shining through the goddess' eyes.

Floating next to the enormous statue Jack peered into the eyes. He could see the crystal jewel set in a rock inside.

"It breaks my heart to damage this artefact, but we have no choice," said Flash. He took out a hammer and chisel and began chipping away at the back of the head where the rock was loose.

The tapping seemed loud under the water. It seemed to disturb the stillness of the temple which had slumbered in silence so long beneath the waves.

Jack and Lara watched as Flash
continued tapping away. After a
while he had made a small hole.
"It will take too long to get all the way
through like this," Flash told them. "I will
have to use a small explosive charge."

"Isn't that dangerous? Didn't you say
the structure might be unstable?"
asked Jack.

"It looks strong enough, if we want the
crystal we'll have to take the chance,"
replied Flash. "We only have ten
minutes of air left before we have to
get back to the sub."

Jack and Lara nodded in agreement.
It was a risk they would have to take.
They both glanced nervously at their
oxygen levels. Ten minutes was not
long.

Chapter 9

The Purple Jewel

Flash put the small explosive charge in the hole he had made with the hammer and chisel and then swam away; indicating to the others that they should also move away and take cover behind a statue.

Flash detonated the charge. Although only a small amount of explosive, the blast through the water was powerful and resonated against the walls inside the enclosed space. Jack and Lara felt the statue they were hiding behind vibrate with the blast. They looked up nervously at the ceiling of the temple, worried that it might collapse. Several stones fell from the walls, tumbling silently through the water onto the floor below, but the temple was strong, and it stayed in one piece.

The three of them swam to the head of the goddess. Flash had used just the right amount of charge to enlarge the hole without damaging the statue too much. Jack was able to reach inside and touch the crystal. It glowed with a soft purple in the darkness.

They had done it! They had reached the fifth crystal, but it was still set in the rock. Flash passed Jack the hammer and the chisel. Jack tapped away, trying to loosen it. Precious seconds ticked by, their oxygen was running lower.

Then with a final tap, the crystal came free. Jack seized it and put it in a pouch at his side. Pointing to the oxygen dial and to the exit he made it clear to the others that they should get out quickly. Time was running out. They swam as fast as they could to the doorway by which they had entered; they swam through - they did not expect what happened next.

Suddenly before them was the enormous head of a giant shark. It opened its mouth and lunged forward, its jaws full of razor-sharp triangular teeth, snapping powerfully, trying to catch them.

"Get back!" Lara screamed in surprise. The three of them, in desperate panic, scrambled backwards; kicking out with their legs. Flash managed to land a kick right on the shark's nose and that bought them a few more seconds to get away, but the shark was not going to give up on such easy prey, it only took moments for it to gather its wits and come after them again.

Jack, Lara and Flash burst into the temple, and in a stream of bubbles they made for the safety of a small gap behind the nearest statue.

The great shark appeared through the doorway. It was over twenty feet long, with a mouth a metre wide. It could easily swallow each one of them whole with no trouble at all, and that was exactly what it intended to do. Attracted by the unusual tapping sound and vibrations it had felt through the water, its finely tuned, predatory instincts were on full alert and it was ready to feed.

Flash, Lara and Jack had managed to hide for a moment, they peered at the shark as it swept powerfully around the temple, but they could not hide for long. The shark's senses were too acute. It homed in on their position, circling at first, and then with a great flick of its tail, it bumped against the statue causing it to wobble.

The three of them tried to keep themselves out of its reach as it came for another pass, snapping with its jaws at Jack's flipper, which he just managed to retract out of reach in time. The shark swam away for a moment, getting ready to attack again. Flash pointed urgently at his oxygen gauge. In their panic about the shark, Jack and Lara had forgotten that they were running out of air. They had to get back to the sub or they would drown. They only had three minutes of oxygen left.

Flash acted quickly. While the shark was away for a few seconds, he swam away from Jack and Lara, pulled an underwater flare from his utility belt and ignited it. It exploded into life, sending out a cascade of bubbles and red light.

Flash swam quickly away from the flare and hid behind another statue.

The shark returned. Attracted to the light and sound of the flare, yet cautious of this unknown oddity, it circled angrily around it, distracted for a moment.

Jack and Lara looked at the doorway to the temple, they would never make it; the shark would spot them as soon as they left their hiding place, and even if they made it through the door, they could never hope to make it all the way along the corridor without it catching them. They were trapped.

Flash meanwhile, swam quickly to the top of the temple while the shark was distracted. He attached an explosive charge and took cover.

The blast shook the whole temple; it was much more powerful than the last explosion. The blast affected the shark, caught in the open, the shock wave knocked it sideways, and its highly tuned senses were momentarily dazed.

Understanding Flash's plan, Jack and Lara forced themselves to recover quickly from the blast. The charge had blown a small hole in the ceiling of the temple, large enough for a human to fit through, but too small for the shark. They swam for it as fast as they could, all the time expecting the shark to come at them from behind; every movement, every breath using up more and more precious oxygen.

They got to the hole, but where was Flash? Jack looked down, and there he was - floating, unconscious, knocked out by the blast. He had been too close to it when it detonated, and he was out cold. Jack and Lara swam back down to him and took him by the shoulders, lifting him towards the hole. Lara swam through first into the brighter waters outside the temple. Then she tried to pull Flash through the hole. Jack pushed from inside the temple. Flash was stuck; his unconscious body now blocked the hole in the roof of the temple.

Jack glanced behind him. The shark was recovering, and now it spotted him. With a flick of its tail, it began to swim with great powerful strokes towards Jack.

Lara heaved at Flash, but it was hard to manoeuvre his unconscious body through the hole. The shark drew closer. Jack pushed with all his might, but Flash's aqualung was caught on the edge of the hole.

Seeing the problem, Lara pulled out her knife, reached in and cut the aqua-lung free, bubbles poured out of the cut tube. Flash had no air, but his body slipped free through the hole, and now both he and Lara were out, floating free above the temple; but Jack was still inside. He glanced below him; the enormous mouth of the shark was wide open, only inches away.

He seized the sides of the hole and propelled himself out with all his might. A tooth of the shark raked down the lower half of his leg as the great jaws closed, but Jack made it out. The huge body of the shark hammered against the roof of the temple behind him.

Now Lara and Jack swam desperately for the mini-sub, supporting Flash between them. Blood trickled from Jack's leg. They only had one minute of oxygen left, and they still had to get into the sub and fill the inside with air. Pulling Flash with them slowed them down, but they were getting closer and closer. Finally they reached the sub and pulled open the canopy. They only had 20 seconds of air left.

They lowered Flash into the sub then climbed in themselves. The oxygen levels on their aqualungs read zero.

Jack could feel it becoming harder and harder to breathe. His lungs screamed for oxygen, but there was none left. He looked at Lara, on her face was an expression of panic as she tried desperately to breathe. With all his last effort Jack pulled shut the canopy and sealed it.

He looked for the control to flood the sub with air. Which was it! Why had he not looked more closely before? Why hadn't he asked Flash about the controls? Their air was gone. Lara began to feel consciousness slipping away from her, her eyes closed; she passed out.

Now it was down to Jack. He reached forward and flicked a switch, hoping to fill the sub with air. It was a guess, unfortunately it was wrong. The sub began moving forward on a collision course with the temple. Jack tried again. He knew that the switch for the oxygen was in this area of the control panel, he was sure. His lungs screamed for air, his vision began to blur. He flicked another switch. This time it was right!

The cabin began to fill with air and

the water to drain away.

However, the mini-sub was still moving forward, and it would only be moments before it collided with the temple.

Jack acted fast, pulling off his own mask, then Lara's, then Flash's, so they could breathe; he lunged for the controls and turned the sub just in time to avoid the temple. He angled the sub towards the surface; it began to ascend, but suddenly with a great jolt it stopped again.

Jack had forgotten that they had tied the sub to the temple with a rope.

Now, with all the aqualung oxygen gone, he had no way to get out of the sub to untie it, besides he couldn't flood the mini-sub with Lara and Flash unconscious.

Jack began to panic, but just then Lara stirred.

"Lara! Lara!" cried Jack. He had never been so pleased that she was ok, "are you alright?" he asked.

"Yes, yes!" said Lara recovering quickly. "I'm ok! I'm ok! What about Flash!"

Jack and Lara leaned over to Flash. "Flash! Flash! wake up!" shouted Lara.

It worked! Flash's eyes began to flicker open in response to her voice. "Lara?" he said still in a daze. Then he opened his eyes, but it was not Lara which he saw, but the fast approaching, open mouth of the giant shark!

"Aargh!" Flash screamed in surprise.

Jack and Lara looked up and saw it too. Jack acted quickly, jolting the controls of the sub sharply to one side. The huge body of the shark passed by, but now it turned around and was heading back. Jack hit full power, but the sub was still tied up. The shark hit with a powerful impact. Crunching and crushing the rear of the vehicle with its mighty jaws; its teeth grating and slicing metal.

The engines moaned in complaint as the mini-sub strained against the nylon rope, the shark opened its mouth wide and bit down hard, piercing the transparent canopy which protected them from the water outside. The freezing ocean began to gush in through the small hole.

The shark opened its mouth again and bit, Lara closed her eyes expecting the end, but then suddenly they were free! The razor-sharp teeth of the shark had sliced through the rope and cut them loose.

The sub shot away towards the surface at maximum speed. The shark was taken by surprise, it had expected sweet flesh, not metal; but now seeing its prey shooting away in a stream of bubbles, it swept after them with powerful strokes of its tail.

Inside the sub, Flash had taken over the controls; water sprayed at him through the hole in the canopy and the deep-sea vehicle was filling up fast. Flash was still dazed and the controls before him swam in and out of focus as the water and dizziness blurred his vision. Jack's leg was bleeding badly from the shark bite. Lara glanced behind at the shark; it was gaining on them rapidly.

"We've got to go faster!" she cried out. Jack and Flash glanced behind them and saw the shark too.

"I'm at full speed!" cried Flash.

The water in the cabin was up to their waists now, and they were still a long way from the surface. The engines of the sub struggled under the strain, smoke and sparks began to erupt from the control panel.

The shark drew closer and closer. It opened its mouth - when suddenly a white object shot past them. It hit the shark head on, bringing it to a sudden stop, as they sped away to the surface they looked back to see the unmistakable shape of 42, standing in the shark's mouth holding open its jaws.

The huge shark thrashed about in frustration and surprise to find its mouth locked open in this way. It forgot its pursuit in its attempts to free itself of this uncomfortable object in its mouth. As Flash, Jack and Lara headed for the surface in the sub they glanced behind them to see the shark and 42, locked in combat disappearing down into the depths.

The mini-sub was now nearly completely full of water. The engines strained as Flash steered it up towards the surface of the ocean high above them.

The three of them prepared to take a last breath and hold it as long as they could. If the engines failed they would never make it; they tilted their heads back to gasp the last of the air inside as the water came up beyond their necks.

"Take a deep breath!" shouted Flash. "I'll blow the canopy!"

They all took a last breath and held it, then Flash pressed the emergency eject button and the canopy of the sub shot away in a cascade of bubbles. They all struggled out of the mini-sub cabin and swam upwards with all their remaining strength.

The sub-engines failed and it began to sink, they were still well below the surface and swimming used up a lot of energy, their lungs were bursting, they were desperate to breathe. Nearly there! They could see the sunshine above the water, a last surge of desperate effort, and they burst out into the fresh air.

They breathed deeply, coughing and spluttering, as they caught their breath, bobbing on the ocean waves.

Flash's crew were quick to help them; a small boat pulled alongside and strong arms pulled the exhausted divers out of the sea. Then suddenly, beside the boat was a giant surge of water; something large was emerging from the waves right next to them. They gasped and turned to see what it was – fully expecting to see the huge, open jaws of the shark ready to engulf them; but it was not the shark, it was the mini-sub.

The submarine rose from the waves, despite its engines being out of action. Flash, Jack and Lara all looked into the water to see how this was possible. Next to the sub was 42!

"The shark is trapped in the temple for the time being," said 42 calmly. "I have rescued the mini-sub, but I suggest we get out of the water quickly before the marine predator returns."

42's calm appraisal of the situation was a sharp contrast to the chaos they had just been through, and they all laughed.

"I think you are right, 42!" smiled Jack.

Flash's crew hauled the sub out of the water. They used a large powerful magnet which swung out on a robotic arm from the side of the ship.

Jack's leg was bandaged, the wound was not bad.

Then the sailors swung the magnet out over 42 and lowered it.

42 was caught by the magnet, the arm was raised and the powerless 42 hung from the metallic arm over the sea.

"Hey! What are you doing?" cried Jack in alarm.

He turned towards Flash, only to find himself face-to-face with the barrel of a laser-pistol.

Flash had them at gun point, and his crew were also armed, their weapons trained on Jack and Lara.

Gone were the smiles and jokes, the sailors levelled their weapons at the crew of the Silver FOX with deadly intent.

"Don't try anything," said Flash in stern warning. "We have your friends."

A group of mean-looking sailors parted to reveal Claws, bound hand and foot and Minnow imprisoned in a golden bird cage.

"Minnow!" he said mournfully, a worried look on his face.

Claws growled at his captors and struggled to get free, but he was held fast.

"We also have your little floating MIM robot sealed in a cabin below," continued Flash. "There is no escape, I suggest you come quietly. We have a lot to talk about."

Flash indicated with his gun that Jack and Lara should enter the Wave Star. They scowled at him, realising they could not get away; exhausted from their ordeal beneath the waves, they allowed themselves to be led below - prisoners of Captain Flash.

Chapter 10

Captives

"I suggest you start telling the truth," said Flash seriously."You went to great lengths to get this crystal," he continued, holding the purple jewel in his hand, turning it over slowly with his fingers. "What is it really for?"

Jack and Lara looked at each other. They had not wanted to risk telling Flash about their quest, but now it seemed they had no choice.

"Go on," nodded Lara. "Tell him."

So Jack told Flash the whole story.

How his village had been attacked ten years ago, how Master Stroud had brought him and Lara up in Truno Abbey, Vendax's attack, his master's death and the Omicron; its jewels and their voyage across the galaxy to find them.

Flash listened intently, his eyes never leaving Jack's face; his laser-pistol continuously at the ready in his hand.

"Well," said Flash, "that's quite a story; and now it's time for me to be honest. My parents are not dead as I implied. We were boarded two days ago by kill-bots; they took us by surprise. They arrested my mother and father and told me that if I ever wanted to see them alive again that I should come to this location, find you, and help you find the crystal. So here's my question: Why did Vendax want me to help you, if you are his enemies?"

There was a moment's silence; then Lara spoke quietly.

"What we have told you is true. I don't know what Vendax is up to, but I do know that we will stop at nothing to destroy him. If he holds your parents captive, perhaps we can help you?"

Flash looked at her, then he began to smile. "I may not have all the answers, but I do know about people, and I know when someone is telling the truth; and you are not lying." He slowly lowered his gun.

"Maybe I'm wrong. Maybe you have fooled me and you really work for Vendax. You do after all have a kill-bot in your crew, and Vendax sent me to help you. However, I trust my feelings. I believe you. If I release you and return your weapons, you and your kill-bot could destroy us all, but I'm willing to take that risk."

Flash's crew looked uneasy, but his broad smile was back again.

"Release them!" he commanded.

"Let's hope that I am right to trust you!" he added looking intently at Jack and Lara.

Flash's crew only hesitated for a moment, and then cut the ropes that bound Claws, who growled and snatched back his weapons. The cage holding Minnow was opened and the little ball of a Fluff jumped free and leapt up onto Jack's shoulder.

"Minnow!" he chirped.

A door was opened at the back of the room and MIM shot free, buzzing about, obviously annoyed at his imprisonment. A great clang on the deck above heralded the return of 42, who stomped down and joined them. Lara and Jack now had their weapons back too. The crew of the Silver FOX were free, and armed. They raised their weapons.

"So - this is where I find out if I was

wrong to trust you," said Flash, looking concerned.

Jack slowly lowered his crossbow; the others put their weapons way too.

"You were not wrong, Flash," Jack said.

"I knew it!" smiled Flash, "I'm sorry to do that to you, but I had to know the truth; I had to find out whose side you were on. These days it is very hard to know who you can trust." Then he looked sad. "I know that Vendax will never release my parents, despite his promises; but if we work together perhaps we can defeat him, and then there might still be a chance to save them; it is the only hope they've got. Come, we have much to discuss."

They were soon gathered round the table; hot drinks warmed them, and now in front of them was the Omicron and the five coloured crystal jewels that they had worked so hard, and risked much, to find.

"So, there is just one more jewel to find," said Flash.

They looked at the galaxy map and found the location of the final crystal that they had to find. Lara tapped the information into the desk computer, and a planet appeared on the screen.

The name of the planet is 'Shard'. It is a barren place, with a large amount of volcanic activity. Settlements are few, and it is very sparsely populated. There are some scientific out-stations which run on geo-thermal energy, drawing power from the heat of the magma which is never far below the surface. It looks like a harsh environment, with thousands of square kilometres covered with solidified lava.

Lara, swung the screen round to show the others. The landscape of Shard was indeed bleak and barren. The twisted, black volcanic rocks spread unbroken for miles and were cracked and split to form sudden jagged trenches and razor-sharp twisted outcrops.

Flash stared at the screen, his face serious.

"Well," he said, "it seems our destinies are more interwoven than we thought. Vendax did not know that my ship had a cloaking-device; I followed his ships to find out where my parents were being held. I have already been to this planet – It is where Vendax is holding my parents."

The Silver FOX crew looked at Flash in surprise. Flash brought up a video on the screen; it was the same barren landscape of Shard that Lara had just showed them, but perched on top of the mountains was a huge white disc-shaped building.

"This is 'Disc Fortress'," explained Flash.

"Its surface is completely smooth, with hidden entry points which will only open for registered transports. There are several squadrons of terror-naught fighters stationed on the disc itself, and five terror-naught super-destroyers which are in orbit directly above it, but those are not its main defences. Covering all approaches by air are these two large guns." A picture of the guns appeared on the screen. "The largest and most deadly in the galaxy; they are able to destroy any object in the air, or in space above the fortress with pin-point accuracy."

"Well, this is going to be easy," said Jack with quiet sarcasm.

"There is more." It was 42's voice. "Before I was re-programmed I was stationed at this fortress. There is a reason it is so well-guarded. It is the centre of all Vendax's operations.

From there he beams all his commands to his kill-bots through a satellite in orbit above the planet. It is the Master Activation Satellite which the terror-naught destroyers and the guns are there to protect."

"This is making me very nervous," said Lara. "First we find out that Vendax knows what we doing, then he sends Flash here to help us, which means he knows where the crystals are, and now we are drawn towards Vendax's own impenetrable fortress, bristling with defences. To me it seems like a trap."

At that moment MIM hovered quietly nearby and landed on the desk next to Minnow who was peering with concern at the screen.

"These MIMs, they can re-produce technology you say?" asked Flash, his face thoughtful.

"Yes," replied Lara. "They are really

quite remarkable."

"I have an idea," said Flash, a smile spreading across his face once more.

"We will need some help, but I think I have a plan; if Vendax has set a trap, perhaps we should spring it, and bring a few surprises of our own."

Chapter 11

Shard

One month later...

The Silver FOX burst out of space-warp above the planet Shard. It was a dark planet with ribbons of glowing, red lava criss-crossing its surface. The thin atmosphere glowed softly in the darkness of space. It was ominous and uninviting. In the cockpit Jack, Lara, Claws, and 42 gazed ahead through the view-screen.

"We've got the signal," said Lara. "Engaging cloak."

"The MIMs did a great job replicating that cloaking technology. Vendax didn't see this coming," smiled Jack as the cloaking device was activated and the Silver FOX disappeared.

"Are you sure they won't be able to detect us?" asked Lara.

"Well, let's hope not, or all this will be for nothing!" replied Jack.

As they descended, they passed through dark, sulphurous clouds and when they finally emerged beneath them, the black, barren landscape of Shard spread out before them. The rocks were black and jagged, noxious mist hung above the broken, blasted ground, and deep chasms dropped away into fiery pits far below the surface. The great cones of giant volcanoes thrust high into the hot air; their peaks were smashed and shattered by ancient eruptions, and inside were deep craters; some dark, empty and bottomless, others smoking and glowing with recent volcanic activity.

"We're approaching the fortress," said Lara.

The Omicron bleeped, the direction arrows pointing the way towards the last crystal jewel, they pointed straight towards Disc Fortress.

"It's as we thought, the last crystal is in the fortress itself," said Jack.

The Silver FOX skimmed low over the hot, shattered surface of Shard. Claws peered down at the dangerous, ragged landscape as it rushed past beneath them. There was no-one on the torn, rocky land below, but had there been, they would have seen and heard nothing of The Silver FOX as it passed. The cloaking device hid them completely, and masked all sound. Their stealthy approach was essential.

Lara steered the little ship low round great, steaming, volcanic mountains, across rivers of red-hot lava which bubbled and oozed as the enormous pressures beneath the surface squeezed molten rock through great canyons which split the crust of the planet.

"There it is!" said Jack suddenly. He pointed forward and they could all see the great, white fortress, built high up in the mountains between three huge volcanic peaks.

It was an enormous, flat, disc-shaped construction, supported in three points by the mountains themselves. The disc hung hundreds of metres above the surface; it was smooth and clean, in stark contrast to the black, cracked rock of the planet on which it was built.

Built on the top of the largest peak which supported the building were the guns. Two huge, gleaming, white thin cylinders pointing skyward; silent, still and ominous; they promised instant obliteration to any ship which dared approach Disc Fortress without permission.

"We're going in," said Lara. She angled the ship towards the peak with the guns.

As they drew closer they began to see the enormous scale of this construction. The disc itself was over ten kilometres wide and the barrels of the guns were at least a kilometre long.

Suddenly the great guns began to move. Smoothly they swivelled to point upwards at an approaching ship which descended from the sky above the disc. A white terror-naught supply shuttle, landing lights blinking, made its steady approach. Had it been an enemy, the giant laser-guns would have picked it out of the sky with one blast, but this shuttle had clearance to land.

It was a large vehicle, with four powerful rocket thrusters at its rear, it was itself huge, and must have weighed thousands of tons, yet as it approached the immense, white disc of the fortress it seemed to shrink to just a tiny, glowing dot. A hangar door opened in the rim of the disc, and the ship disappeared inside. Then the door-way closed, and the disc was again smooth and perfect.

Lara brought The Silver FOX around the mountain which held the guns. Its sides were steep, but towards the top was a ledge, just wide enough for her to set the ship down for a moment. They were perilously close to the edge, and one false move would mean their instant destruction, and the end of all their plans before they had even begun.

Claws was at the service-ramp, he clicked the switch and the door opened. Hot, sulphurous air blasted in from the outside and Claws staggered back raising two arms on one side of his body to defend against the blast. He wore tinted protective goggles over his eyes to protect him from the heat and a face mask to filter out the noxious fumes. His surprise was only momentary. He recovered his composure and gave a thumbs-up sign to Lara and Jack.

He jumped from the ramp, and immediately began to climb the vertical, ragged cliff which rose thousands of metres straight up towards the giant guns.

On each of his six paws he wore silver heat-proof gloves. Claws was an excellent climber, and he threw himself into this climb with all the feline strength and agility at his disposal.

Lara and the others watched anxiously as he ascended the huge cliff. Over his shoulders he had a harness, and attached to that was a strong, thin, silver rope. The rope trailed behind him, then out, and up, and into the open hatch-way of the Silver FOX. There Jack stood, dressed in similar protective goggles and gloves and wearing a silver suit to reflect the heat, he watched Claws, feeding the line out as the cat climbed. Lara was at the controls of the Silver FOX. As Claws ascended the mountain she skillfully hovered the ship so that it stayed level with their cat companion in his dangerous climb.

Lara matched pace with Claws perfectly, and gradually the cat and the Silver FOX, with a thin, metal line strung between them, rose silently up the side of the mountain towards the edge of Disc Fortress and the giant guns high above.

Chapter 12

Flash

Captain Flash, at the controls of the cloaked Wave Star, piloted his ship low over the barren surface of Shard until he too saw the huge, white Disc Fortress suspended between the three enormous volcanic peaks.

He looked up at the great guns which pointed skyward, defending the impenetrable round citadel from attack from the air. He looked towards the base of the mountain on which the guns stood, but he saw nothing. He knew though, that the Silver FOX and her crew must be in position by now, that Claws must have begun his perilous climb. It was

good that they could not be seen.
He had a different mission. He angled
the Wave Star away from the guns
and flew instead towards the disc
itself. Still keeping low, and now
reducing his speed to a minimum, he
approached the huge, round, smooth
surface of the disc.

He watched as the large supply
shuttle approached the disc and
disappeared into a small opening
which appeared as if from nowhere
on its seamless side.

Flash nodded, a slight smile appeared
for a moment on his lips, the plan was
working, and then he frowned in
concentration again as he brought his
attention back to the task in hand.

He took the Wave Star right along the
edge of the disc to a point not far
from where it was supported by the
second mountain peak, a point as far
from the guns as possible.

The Wave Star hovered in position. Flash's heart beat fast at the thought of being so close to Disc Fortress. One false move and the alarm would be raised; hundreds of terror-naught fighters would burst out of their hangars around the rim of the disc, and hopelessly out-numbered, and out-gunned it would mean the end of him, the Wave Star and its crew. It would also mean the end of all their hopes to destroy Vendax. Stealth was essential.

"Ready," he whispered to his crew-mate. He knew he didn't have to whisper, but somehow it felt that they were so close to the disc that even their words might be heard.

Inside the disc, a young officer in a pristine uniform and shining black jack-boots looked with concern at his console.

"Sir," said the eager young officer.

His superior commander was also immaculately dressed, but his face told a different story to that of the younger soldier before him; his eyes were tired, his face lined. He had seen too much war, and his retirement could not come too soon.

"What is it?" said the commander. He didn't try to keep the annoyance out of his voice. He was fed up with this stream of enthusiastic new recruits who were desperate for action, for promotion, but who usually only found a quick death.

"Sir, I've picked up some strange readings. There are fluctuations in the magnetic field around the disc in this area here." The junior officer pointed at the computer screen, a soft, small green blur showed up just in the area where the Wave Star was positioned.

The commander peered at the screen, then leaned back, and looked disdainfully at the junior officer.

"We are perched on top of a volcano," frowned the commander "All we get is one, great, long fluctuation in - everything. Strange readings here; are not a strange thing."

"But sir..." began the junior officer.

His commander interrupted him. "Listen, it's nothing; don't be so eager to find something wrong. Let the robots worry about things like that, we are just here to press buttons when we're told too." Then he laughed scornfully – "I tell you what, if someone attacks the disc let me know! Otherwise I'm not to be disturbed."

The commander stomped away, his boots clicking on the white metal floor; his thoughts on a green bottle of Tabrian Brandy which he had hidden in the back of his desk drawer.

The junior officer frowned. He was sure that this was something. He returned to the console and continued to monitor the fluctuations.

In the Wave Star outside, Flash had no idea that at least one person inside knew he was there. All he could do was pray that he could deliver his special packages, and get away fast.

A MIM floated in the air before him. Flash held a small white disc. He tapped the controls at the side, and a very small light began to flash with a quiet beep.

"Ok," said Flash."It's armed. The timer is set. There is no going back now." He added half to himself.

The MIM bleeped as if in reply, extended its robotic arms and took hold of the device. Then turning full circle in the air he flew towards a small open hatch way in the side of the Wave Star.

The MIM flew out into the blustery air

high above the volcanic wasteland below. The little robot was buffeted this way and that, and it beeped in alarm as a strong gust of hot air pushed it suddenly towards the edge of the disc. If it smashed against the fortress it could be detected and the game would be up; but it just managed to get control in time using the little thrusters on either side of its body to stabilise its position. For a moment the winds dropped and now the MIM hovered steadily towards the smooth surface of the disc. In its robotic arm the small, white device.

Closer and closer the MIM drew towards the disc, and then delicately it placed the explosive device onto the side of the fortress. The mine was magnetised and stuck there; small and almost completely invisible on the surface of the disc. MIM turned and hovered back towards the Wave Star.

With MIM safely back on board, Flash sighed with relief.

"OK, well done! – One down, ninety nine to go!" he exhaled.

He eased the cloaked Wave Star along the side of Disc Fortress and repeated the process; leaving small explosive devices at regular intervals along its side. It took a while, but eventually all the explosive charges were in place.

"Right, job done!" smiled Flash at the MIM which bleeped happily.
"That ought to give them something to think about! Time to meet the others; the count-down has begun. Let's get this party started!"

Flash accelerated away, and then angled the Wave Star up towards space.

Inside Disc Fortress the junior officer watched his console. The green blur which had been worrying him slowly faded away, but his doubts still lingered. He was sure something was wrong, but now all the readings were normal. He stepped back, rested his hand on the leather holster of his laser pistol and frowned.

Who was he kidding? - this was a dead-end assignment. Nothing ever happened here.

Chapter 13

42

The shuttle came out of space-fold and approached the planet Shard. Before it were five terror-naught super-destroyers; immense, white, armoured space-ships, each one the size of a city, hanging in the blackness of space.

"Shuttle 3874C, requesting permission to land," said the captain of the shuttle into his inter-com.

"Permission granted," came the crackling reply from the radio speakers. "You may start your approach."

The shuttle was not an elegant ship - it was designed to carry as much as possible, not to look good; but its engines were powerful, and despite its heavy pay-load, it quickly and smoothly entered the atmosphere of Shard and began to descend.

It was not long before the pilot spotted the large white disc which was the shuttle's destination. He had made this trip many times, but it still unnerved him the way those huge guns swung round to track his descent.

The shuttle approached the edge of the disc.

"Shuttle 3874C, permission granted to enter disc." A voice crackled over the radio.

A small section of the side of the huge white disc slid open to reveal a cargo bay, and the shuttle, dwarfed by the size of the enormous white fortress, disappeared inside.

The cargo-hangar doors slid shut behind the shuttle as it landed smoothly, and its rear doors opened.

A flurry of activity began. Technicians swarmed over the vehicle, re-fuelling pipes were attached and important functions checked. Hover-vehicles moved into position and started unloading cargo and supplies.

On a world as remote as this, everything had to be flown in, and the arrival of the shuttle was a regular occurrence. No-one gave a second glance to the centurion kill-bot walking calmly down the service-ramp out of the shuttle. Behind him hovered several containers. He walked slowly and confidently out of the cargo-bay with his supplies, and followed the long corridor around the edge of the disc.

No-one noticed a tiny pair of eyes

peeping through a crack in one of the containers. No-one heard the quiet voice which came from within.

"Minnow!" it whispered nervously.

In his hand the kill-bot held a small device with crystal jewels inserted in holes around the outside. It bleeped softly, a glowing arrow pointed in the direction he was walking.

42 couldn't smile, but he would have done if he could. The plan was working; the crystal was near; so far, so good.

Chapter 14

The Guns

Claws had climbed high up the side of the mountain now. He was quick and agile, a human could never have made this climb, and no-one expected that anyone would ever try. The approach to the guns was completely undefended. Exhausted and hot, Claws finally reached the smooth white dish in which the guns where mounted. He peered cautiously over the edge.

A kill-bot sentry stood guard. He was standing close to where Claws clung to the cliff. This was unexpected; they had hoped that the gun dish would be deserted as they were remotely controlled from inside Disc Fortress.

Suddenly, something caught the kill-bot's attention. He marched forward and stared at where the Silver FOX hovered cloaked.

Jack had closed the hatch on the side of the Silver FOX, except for a tiny crack through which hung the rope, and through which Jack now also aimed his cross-bow. - The kill-bot could see the silver rope, apparently floating in mid-air. He leaned forward and looked again, uncertain of what he was seeing.

Jack shot, the blast hit the robot's eyes, confusing it and throwing it off balance. At the same moment Claws leaped up, grabbed the kill-bot's arm and pulled it hard. The kill-bot bounced off the side of the mountain as he fell; he smashed into the jagged black rocks far below and lay there in a twisted wreck of white metal. Claws acted quickly. He jumped up

over the side of the gun
emplacement and secured the rope.

Jack attached a package to the line
and let it slide down. Claws caught it
and detached it from the line. Jack
sent another package, and again
Claws caught it and detached it.

Claws opened the packages and
inside were the high explosives
encased in small, white magnetic
discs. These he began to attach
around the base of the guns. He
placed them at key structural points,
until at last he was satisfied that they
would do enough damage.

He then returned to the rope and tied
it to his harness. He gave Jack a
thumbs-up sign and the Silver FOX
lifted away, carrying Claws with it,
hanging from the line.

Jack hit a switch, and the rope began
to be winched in. Claws rose up to
the doorway of the Silver FOX and

Jack helped the exhausted cat on board.

"Ok!" said Jack to Lara. "He's on board. Let's go!"

Chapter 15

Into the Disc

42 walked down another long, white corridor following the directions shown him by the Omicron. He knew he was close to the crystal jewel and now it was time to let the others in.

He opened one of the containers he had brought with him and took out a laser-cutting torch. He aimed it at the ceiling and turned it on to full power. The white ceiling above him glowed red-hot as the metal began to melt. He moved the torch in a circle and cut a neat hole. The metal he had cut away smashed to the floor and daylight shone through the hole.
As the Silver FOX approached the top

of the disc they could clearly see the hole 42 had cut, and Lara made straight for it and landed the ship gently over the round opening, concealing it with the cloaked Silver FOX from anyone who might happen look down from above.

Jack, Lara and Claws sprang into action, down the service-ramp, under the invisible Silver FOX and down the hole. Their luck had lasted this far, but it couldn't hold much longer, they must act quickly if they were to get the crystal without being caught. 42 let Minnow out of one of the containers and he clambered up onto Jack's shoulder. 42 passed Jack the Omicron, and they all looked at the arrows.

Drawing their weapons they silently followed the direction it showed them; it was pointing towards the centre of Disc Fortress, but the corridor they were on just circled round the outside, they had to find a way in through the wall on their right.

At last there was a door, but it was
locked. 42 smashed the lock panel,
and Jack got to work on the wires,
Lara tapped on the computer keys;
something worked. The door opened.
They entered, and found themselves
on a balcony overlooking the most
incredible and horrifying view that
any of them had ever seen.

They stood high on the edge of a
huge chamber which completely
filled the huge interior of Disc Fortress.
Stretching away before them to the
centre of the disc was row, upon row
of cylindrical glass tubes. They were
stacked at least a hundred high and
were laid out in great circles fanning
out from the disc's centre. The tubes
were each rounded off with metal
top and bottom; they were filled with
a clear liquid. Inside each tube was a
person.

The people inside the tubes hung,

pale and motionless; naked except for simple undergarments, most had eyes closed, but others stared eerily through the glass. Their unmoving faces frozen in one expression; tubes and wires were connected to the bodies, and through these, coloured liquids moved and soft lights occasionally glowed.

"What is this place?" Lara whispered in horror.

"Why would they keep the dead like this?" asked Jack.

"Sir," said 42's deep voice. "They are not dead. They are alive."

Jack and Lara turned to 42 in surprise. "What?" gasped Jack.

42 pointed to a tube near to them, at its base was some sort of life support monitor. As they all looked they could clearly see a slow, but steady heartbeat being registered.

Minnow clung to Jack's shoulders.

"Minnow" he said in fear.

The whole place had an ominous feel.
The people in the tubes looked
vulnerable, helpless; the living dead.

The Omicron continued to bleep softly
and the arrows on its surface pointed
the way to the final crystal jewel and
the end of their quest. They pointed
directly to the centre of the rows the
glass tubes, the centre of Disc Fortress.

Chapter 16

Centre of the Disc

A metal spiral staircase circled down to the floor of the chamber. The companions descended it and found themselves in a long, thin corridor, on either side of which were the glass tubes containing the motionless bodies.

The bodies inside hung eerily in the clear liquid within the tubes. They were close by on either side, they stretched as far as the eye could see into the distance and they were stacked high above them. They were completely surrounded by hundreds of thousands of the unconscious bodies.

"I don't like this place," whispered Lara.

Claws growled in agreement.

"Let's get to the crystal as soon as possible," replied Jack.

"Minnow," said Minnow in agreement.

It took them a long time to reach the centre of the Disc Fortress. The Omicron constantly confirmed that they were heading the right way, bleeping with increased intensity and speed to show that they were very close to the final crystal jewel now.

Suddenly, Lara stopped. She was staring at a body in one of the tubes; slowly, she raised her hands to the glass. The person inside was one of her kind, with blue skin and pointed ears just like hers. Tears filled Lara's eyes. Jack stood behind her and put his hand reassuringly on her shoulder. Lara did not know any of her people, she had thought she was the only one of her kind, and now she had finally found someone of her own race - but what a place to find them.

The companions all stopped and stood with Lara; then they looked up and about them and saw that this blue body was not alone; there were hundreds of blue bodies stretching high above and around them.

"My people," gasped Lara at last. "So this is where they were taken."

A look of fierce determination fixed itself onto Lara's face; she turned towards the centre of the disc. "Come on," she said. "Let's do this."

Increasing their pace to match Lara's determined stride, they finally reached the end of the corridor of tubes. All the rows of bio-tubes spread out in concentric circles from this point to the edge of the disc; this was the very centre of Disc Fortress; the centre of this horrific warehouse of bodies. The corridor they were in ended in a short flight of stairs which they climbed and found themselves on the edge of a large, circular platform about hundred metres in diameter.

The platform was empty, except for three objects; two cylindrical tubes covered in a white fabric, and between them right at the very centre of the platform a large, black rectangular block. The Omicron arrows pointed directly towards the rectangular object. Cautiously the companions approached.

As they drew nearer, they could see that set right in the very middle of the rectangle was the final blue crystal jewel. It glowed softly with a pale inner light which made it stand out clearly against the black background on which it was mounted. Jack approached, Lara and Claws on either side, Minnow on his shoulder, 42 behind. This was it. They had found the final jewel for the Omicron.

Jack reached out and touched the jewel. It came away easily and he held it with the tips of his fingers, savouring the moment, letting the others see it too.

42 lifted the Omicron, and Jack placed the final jewel in position. It slotted neatly into place, with a soft click.

After all they been through, this was the moment they had waited for. They stared at the Omicron, waiting for something to happen. Nothing did.

Then suddenly, there came a sound; the clang of two metal objects banging against each other. The sound came from somewhere very close. Clang! Clang! It seemed to come from just behind the black rectangular object in front of them. The sound continued in a steady, ominous rhythm.

Then slowly, the black object began to turn; as it did the companions drew back. Their mouths dropped open in surprise. Claws hissed through his sharp teeth, Minnow squealed in alarm. Hearts pounding, they all reached for their weapons.

The object from which they had taken the crystal was in fact the back of a large, black chair. Now the chair was turning round to face them, and sitting in the chair, resplendent in his perfect white armour, was Vendax himself.

It was him that was making the metallic sound - he was slowly clapping.

Chapter 17

Vendax

"Well done! Well done!" boomed Vendax's powerful robotic voice.

His black eyes stared unblinking at them. His huge, white, metal body sat easily in the chair, his long cloak flowing down behind him. As always on his lips was frozen a sinister, enigmatic smile. Jack, Lara and the others starred in horrified surprise.

From behind Vendax emerged a squad of kill-bots. They quickly spread out around the platform and surrounded the crew of the Silver FOX. It was hopeless. Out-numbered and out-gunned, Jack, Lara and Claws lowered their weapons in surrender.

"Congratulations!" continued Vendax.
"What a show you have put on for us!"

"What do you mean?" asked Jack. His
voice sounded small.

"You have found all the crystal jewels
for the Omicron, and my, what a
journey you have had! You have
travelled right the way across the
galaxy! What adventures! - Battles
with giant spiders, dragons, scorpions,
snakes and killer sharks! Most
entertaining! – Yes, we really have
enjoyed the show."

With that, from the ceiling a large
screen was slowly lowered, and on it
were projected images of Jack and
the others from their different
adventures across the galaxy -
climbing Spire Mountain and fighting
the giant spiders on planet Doom,
then being chased across the ice by
the snow-creatures and ice-birds,
then battling the sandvipers and the
shark in the underwater temple –

154

everything had been filmed, everything had been watched.

"Yes!" spat Vendax. We have watched you the whole time! I really didn't think you would make it at points, I thought the sandvipers would be the end of you for sure! We really have enjoyed it, haven't we my good friends, John and Mary."

Vendax waved his hands at the covered cylinders on either side of his chair; as he did so, the covers lifted, drawn away from above. Inside one tube was a man, and in the other a woman. They were motionless, suspended in the clear liquid, just like all the other bodies in the giant chamber. Jack recognised them instantly. His face went pale.

"Mum? Dad?" he whispered.

"Yes," sneered Vendax, "John and Mary Trainer; 'Mum and Dad'. They have really enjoyed watching your adventures. They can't move or speak - but they can still see and hear."

Jack moved forward to the cylinders reaching out with trembling fingers. He stared at his mother and his father, their eyes open, they stared back at him, but they were paralysed and motionless.

"What have you done to them?" he shouted at Vendax. "You monster!"

"Monster? Monster?" mocked Vendax. "Am I the monster? Who do you think invented the kill-bots? Not me – no! It was your father! It was 'Dad' that invented these, oh so, - 'evil' machines!" Vendax laughed.

Jack looked at Vendax in horror.

"Yes, your father invented the technology which made the kill-bots possible. Of course he did not have the ambition to see their true military potential; he invented a medical robot, a machine into which a mind could be placed. It was to be the saviour of those whose bodies were injured beyond repair. They would have a chance to live again. Their brain would be connected to the 'med-bot' and their mind would be alive in the body of a robot. Oh yes, and John soon had a chance to try out his technology didn't he? Yes – it was me he tried it out on! I had an accident, my body smashed and broken, I should have been dead, but John Trainer - your father, decided to try his new technology out on me. It was he who made me. This suit -" Vendax waved his hand over his metallic body, "this is the original med-bot suit that he made for me!"

Jack was so stunned he didn't know what to say. He stood and stared at his mother and father, they had not changed, not aged a day since he had last seen them.

Vendax continued - "But they weren't

ready were they?" He hissed. "No, they were not ready for a long time. Five years! Five Years! It took for them to get the technology complete. In all that time I hung in the glass tube, naked and alone, they thought I was unconscious, but the drugs they gave me were administered in much too high doses, and in all that time, for five long years I could I see, and hear, and feel, and think, but never sleep, never rest. It was enough to drive anyone - quite mad!" Vendax giggled insanely.

"Yes, I could see, and hear," whispered Vendax, suddenly quiet as he stood and walked up to the tube containing Jack's mother and stared at her face. "I could see her looking at him, and I could see him beginning to fall for her. I had to watch the first time they kissed. She knew the way I felt about her, yet she stood before me and kissed him. Then as I hung there powerless, I watched their love grow; they married and then - a child was born."

Vendax turned and looked down at Jack - "Yes," he said. "You were that child. I promised myself as I hung there, in pain, in physical and mental anguish, that I would have revenge. One day I would make John and Mary, my 'friends', suffer, the way they had made me suffer."

Vendax paused. The chamber was silent. Then in a steady voice, filled with dangerous malice, he continued.

"So - finally they were ready, they connected my brain to this robotic body, but I was ready too. I seized control of this medical facility and changed the technology for my own purposes. I had always seen the greater potential for this invention. I turned my own version of your father's med-bot into the kill-bots that you know so well - I had an army!

My machines were much simpler to manufacture, the brain of the host only needed to be partially connected; no need for more complex brain functions, no need for independent thought and feelings like love, compassion, understanding; I only needed the host for the most basic life functions - the rest I could control. With chemicals and computer programs, I was able to boost their aggression, their determination, their ruthlessness, and their loyalty.

I already had hundreds of bodies ready to connect to the kill-bots, but I needed more. So I sent my kill-bots to attack and capture more bodies, and I turned those people into more kill-bots and then I sent them out to get more people, and turned them into kill-bots and so on and so on! Look around you! Wasn't it effective? – What a system! – Nothing could stop me!" Vendax extended his arms to indicate the bodies which filled the huge chamber inside Disc Fortress. "Each and every body in these tubes is a kill-bot!"

Jack, Lara and Claws gazed around them in horror.

"Yes - those evil robots you hate so much, are actually people! I have millions of bodies and I have millions of kill-bots. They don't know what they are doing of course; I don't want robots which can think! I provide the orders, and they carry them out without question! If a kill-bot is destroyed I just replace the machine, – the person powering it is unharmed and ready to be plugged into another kill-bot. I have made all these people immortal! They will endlessly fight for me, until I have complete control of the whole galaxy! And this is just the beginning; soon I will build more discs just like this one and I will fill them with bodies for my kill-bots. The volcanic activity of this planet will provide all the geo-thermal energy I will ever need. One day everyone will be a machine. It is perfect! I am unstoppable!" shouted Vendax, "Yes, my kill-bots and I will live forever! I have become - a God!"

Then the great, white robot stopped, and his voice lowered again.

"Yet - with all this power, one can become, well - bored. It's too easy you see. No challenge. But then there was you, Jack. Looking forward to this moment has kept me going over the years, Jack."

Vendax now turned and spoke to Jack's parents.

"What a boy! In your absence, 'Mum and Dad'- I arranged his up-bringing! Yes!" Vendax span and pointed at Jack. "It was I who arranged for you to be taken to Truno Abbey. It was I who made sure you were trained in the art of combat and given the mental and physical skills to be able to complete this voyage across the galaxy. I wanted some real entertainment, not just someone who would fall at the first hurdle. It was I who hid the crystal jewels. I chose dangerous places in which to put them and then chemically enhanced the creatures that lived nearby to be more dangerous. I placed hundreds of cameras at each location and watched you by satellite from far above - what entertainment! It was quite a project I can tell you! It took years to set up!"

As Vendax ranted on, the companions all listened in crushed silence.

"The sad thing is, that you believed it all!" said Vendax with a mocking laugh. "Did you really believe that the Omicron would save you? Gathering crystal jewels for an ancient device? Some sort of magic perhaps? This is reality, Jack, not a fairy tale from one of your library books. I organised the whole thing. I allowed your Master Stroud - the fool - to discover the Omicron. I allowed you to escape on the Silver FOX - you think it was a coincidence that it just happened to be there, ready for you? I could have destroyed you at any moment.

Jack looked once more at his mother and father. At last he had found them, he never thought he would see them again, he thought they were dead, but to find them like this, at the mercy of this insane robot.

Vendax looked at the companions. They stood small before him, they looked defeated; all they had believed in had come to nothing.

"Lara!" Vendax spoke so suddenly, that Lara jumped. "You thought you were alone in the universe didn't you? The only little blue girl in the galaxy? - Well you are not - I conquered your world, I took your people, I made them all kill-bots. You have seen them in my tubes haven't you?"

Tears came to Lara's eyes. She had always been alone and it was Vendax who was responsible.

"Oh, don't cry my dear," said Vendax with mock concern. "You will soon be joining them!"

"And you - cat! -'Claws!' – really what a ridiculous name! Your people will soon be just a memory; I have a new fleet ready to attack your planet, and this time your puny defences will be of no use; in one blow, I will wipe out all life on your world. I know, I know - it's just evil isn't it? But I'm afraid that 'evil' is just the kind of guy I am!"

Vendax laughed, then slowly his laughter died away, and his voice sounded mournful.

"And now, I almost feel sad," he continued. "It is all nearly over - my great game! There is, of course, the final, best part to come. The part I have been really waiting for. Can you imagine how your parents felt every time they saw you in danger, how terrified they must have been, how scared for you. That was my torture for them, my revenge for what they did to me; but it was not enough, not nearly enough! I want them to watch as you and your friends join my ranks. Yes, today your parents will watch as each one of you is inserted into your own tube, as each one of you becomes one of my kill-bots!"

Chapter 18

The Chip

"That's quite a story," said Jack quietly. "Let me tell you a story of my own."

Vendax stopped and looked at Jack. He had not expected this. He laughed softly and sat down in his chair. "Please - why not? Go ahead. Tell us your 'story'." Vendax's voice was laced with scorn.

"My story is about a certain young Captain Flash. You captured his ship and kidnapped his parents to make him help us. You knew we would need him to get the purple crystal from the underwater temple, but what you didn't know was that Flash had a ship with a cloaking-device."

Vendax slowly sat up. Jack had got his attention.

"A cloaking-device? That technology is just a myth. It doesn't exist, it's just..." began Vendax.

"...a fairy tale?" finished Jack. "Yes, Vendax, Flash and his parents were archaeologists, they looked for old technology - and they found it. An ancient device from an old civilization which could hide a whole ship, make it invisible to the eye and to sensors. Flash followed you in his cloaked ship. He followed you here. He knew you were holding his parents here. Yes - Flash knew all about ancient technology, he knew enough to work out that the Omicron was a fake.

Yes, Vendax, we worked it out! We knew that the Omicron would do nothing; we knew it was just a way to lure us here to you. Why else would you get Flash to help us? Why would you not just destroy us when you had the chance as we landed vulnerable on the ocean before we met Flash? How could you always have been so close on our trail unless you knew where we were going? Unless - you had planned it all?

Flash studied the map you had put on the Omicron and he saw that the location of the final crystal jewel was here on Shard. We traced the signal here to this Disc Fortress. We knew that this was where you would be waiting.

We didn't come here today to find the final crystal jewel for the Omicron. We came to destroy you!"

Vendax laughed. He waved his hand towards the kill-bots that surrounded them.

"And how pray do you propose to do that?" he asked.

"The Omicron itself may have been a fake, but our galaxy voyage in search of the crystal jewels caused us to meet many people; brave people; people who you have hurt; people who are now our friends; people who would do anything to stop you. Your game has backfired on you, Vendax. The Omicron did unlock a powerful weapon. All of us! The Omicron brought us together, against you!"

Jack walked up to Vendax. Suddenly he did not seem defeated, but confident. Vendax just sat motionless, silently listening.

Jack continued. "Yes, you have millions of people imprisoned here on this world. Each person is a kill-bot in your army, as a force they are unbeatable; but there is a flaw in your plan. The kill-bots have to be linked to the bodies here on the planet, or else they cannot function, and the whole system relies on just one satellite uplink. What if that satellite uplink were broken? What if the Master Activation Satellite were destroyed?"

"Ha! Impossible!" spat Vendax. "The satellite is defended by five of my most powerful destroyers as well as the disc guns. Hundreds of terror-naught fighters patrol the area! No ship could even get close!"

"Not even a cloaked ship?" asked Jack.

His question hung in the silence.

"Huh!" laughed Vendax scornfully, although Jack had clearly worried him, "You and your 'friends' don't stand a chance! Aren't you forgetting your current predicament?" Vendax again waved his hand to indicate the kill-bots which surrounded them.

"I'm hoping," smiled Jack. "that we have thought of everything..."

Just then, there was a humming noise,

the sound of many small engines all
approaching at full speed.

"Meet some of our friends," said Jack
calmly.

Suddenly the air was full of MIMs and
riding them were the Minnow-kind!
Small fluffy creatures, like Minnow, but
with fur of a whole range of different
colours and now the MIMs and their
fluffy riders buzzed and whizzed in
sudden chaos in the air around them.
It was impossible to count them, but
there must have been thirty or forty of
the fluffy creatures on their robot
steeds.

"Minnow!!!!" they cried as they
zoomed through air flying on their
MIMs.

As they passed the kill-bots, they
dropped little white magnetic discs
onto the robots' backs and then
whizzed away so fast that they were
just a blur.

The kill-bots had no time to react; they were taken completely by surprise. The little creatures had been hidden in 42's cargo crates along with their newly created MIMs. They were brave and skillful. Each magnetic disc they had dropped on the kill-bots was an explosive device, and now the explosions began.

Each disc blasted inwards, shattering the insides of the kill-bot it was attached to. Some of the robots tried to remove the explosive discs, but they were too small for the robots' broad hands. Other kill-bots began blasting at the Minnows, but the MIMs were too quick. The kill-bots fell, one after the other.

Vendax rose slowly from his chair, raised himself to his full height and towered over Jack.

"Impudent wretch!" he uttered in a deep threatening tone.

Then 42 came to life, and in a sudden move he leapt at Vendax and landed on his back, clamping his metal arm around his neck.

Vendax swung violently this way and that, trying to throw 42 off, but 42 hung on tightly, and with his other hand he tapped the buttons on a control panel which was between Vendax's shoulder blades.

Vendax tried to reach around to grab 42, and he had nearly got hold of him. Lara leapt forward igniting her laser spear and slashed at Vendax's arm. The laser-tipped weapon sparked against the armour, and the attack distracted Vendax, but as soon as the laser was drawn away, the metal healed itself and Vendax was undamaged.

Jack and Claws joined the fight, blasting with crossbow and pistols at Vendax's head; confused for a moment Vendax staggered, but again was undamaged.

42 hung on, and now he had gained access to the inside of Vendax's armour. He reached in and took hold of a small computer chip, he managed to rip it free, then with a powerful twist Vendax threw 42 off and he smashed to the ground.

The Minnow and MIMs were ready to attack with their limpet mines; they hung in the air, ready to surge forward and attach all their explosives. Lara held her laser-spear, Jack and Claws levelled their guns at the giant white robot, all were prepared to die to destroy this evil machine.

"Wait..." said 42.

Chapter 19

Master Activation Satellite

In space far above the planet Shard, the five giant terror-naught destroyers hung in space, protectors of the satellite which beamed commands to kill-bots all over the galaxy.

They had no idea an attack would come, and when it did they were utterly unprepared.

Captain Flash drew the cloaked Wave Star close to the terror-naughts, and then gave the signal.

"All ships, attack now!" he commanded into his intercom. All at once a motley host of ships disengaged their cloaking devices and began attacking the terror-naughts at point blank range.

Captain Flash had his own sailors following him in the assault. They flew small, fast fighters coloured bronze and red, nipping quickly around the kill-bot ships, blasting key vulnerable points and then re-cloaking.

Also in the assault were Kendra and her people. Their ships were customised by the MIMs, parts from other ships found in scrap yards, bonded together, not aero-dynamic but deadly effective, they had utilised all the best parts of ships they had cannibalised. Some carried huge cumbersome weapons that seemed too large for the vehicle they were attached to. They de-cloaked just long enough to deliver a huge, deadly pay-load, and then jettisoned the clumsy, yet powerful weapon, re-cloaked and disappeared.

Also in the battle were the fast, high-tech ships of Claws' people - the Clorn-Ardua. They piloted their smooth, rounded blue and white, light-weight fighters with great skill, and they already had experience at fighting terror-naughts from the battle at Duatha. Fast, and armed with missiles and lasers, the cat-ships streaked through the battle-zone picking off stray terror-naught fighters and delivering perfectly placed missiles into the huge kill-bot destroyers, crippling their weapons systems, smashing their communication arrays and destroying the activation spheres which controlled their terror-naught fighters. Their weapons were powerful, and were fired with deadly accuracy.

Lasers of every colour slashed across the darkness of space and sliced into the kill-bot ships. Before the kill-bots had time to fire, major systems were destroyed; the huge terror-naught super-destroyers began exploding in giant yellow and red eruptions of flame.

Cloaked ships appeared from no-where, delivered a missile and a hail of laser fire and then disappeared before the kill-bots could retaliate.

Some terror-naught fighters began to give chase, but the ships they pursued just disappeared, and another cloaked ship suddenly materialised from an unexpected quarter and blasted them into fiery destruction.

The giant guns above Disc Fortress swivelled round and aimed in the direction of the cloaked ships, they angled upwards and made ready to fire. Even at this distance they could cause devastating damage and a steady stream of fire could cover a vast area of space above, eventually they would destroy all the cloaked ships, even if it meant hitting their own ships too; at least the satellite would be safe.

"Ready to fire!" ordered the gun commander.

"Fire!" he shouted.

But the guns never fired. Instead the mines that Claws had planted exploded, with impeccable timing; ripping and smashing the base of the gun barrels in a roar of flame. The gun emplacement collapsed and the giant guns fell, crashing down the side of the mountain, breaking as they smashed against the hard, black volcanic rock, and finally, impacting on the surface of Disc Fortress itself they skidded in broken pieces across its smooth, white surface.

In the Disc Command Centre, the eager junior officer burst into his commander's office.

"Sir, you asked me only to disturb you if we were being attacked! - Well, we are being attacked!"

The commander's face was a picture of surprise and horror. The brandy bottle dropped from his hand.

"What....?" began the commander.

Now, the mines that Flash had planted against the side of Disc Fortress detonated too.

In a giant explosion, the junior officer and his commander both disappeared, along, with the whole of the commander's office, and the bottle of brandy, out of the side of the disc and down onto the volcanic rocks below.

On Disc Fortress, chaos was total. Human guards and kill-bots alike, ran about without order or direction.

Escape pods were jettisoned as personnel sought to escape the burning, and now undefended Fortress.

The docking bays of the disc opened and white terror-naught fighters blasted out, screaming up into the sky to join the battle, but it was already too late.

The surprise had been total, and the five terror-naught super-destroyers above the planet were now just flaming wrecks, smashed and powerless, the few remaining kill-bot fighters were picked off by bright flashes of laser blasts from de-cloaking ships. Flash and his ramshackle fleet were hardly damaged at all.

Now the Wave Star de-cloaked and flanked by two other sleek, powerful pirate ships, it streaked through the night sky towards the unprotected Master Activation Satellite. With bright blue flashes they each launched two missiles which sped away, trailing white smoke behind them.

The missiles impacted against the satellite and it crumpled and then exploded in a bright, yellow flower of destruction; metal fragments span off in every direction and the satellite disintegrated and disappeared, leaving only shattered debris.

The signal connecting the bodies in Disc Fortress on the planet below to kill-bots across the galaxy was cut.

Kill-bots everywhere simply froze. With no life force, no brain to activate them, they were just useless hunks of metal. Vendax's army was no more.

Chapter 20

Dax

Vendax stared at the view-screen and watched as his fleet was destroyed. He watched the guns collapse and fall; he watched the fires erupt all round the edge of Disc Fortress and he watched as the satellite, with which he controlled his world, disintegrated in a ball of flame.

One moment he had commanded an army of millions across the galaxy, the next there was nothing, but him. The kill-bots on the platform lay destroyed by the Minnow-kind.

Jack and Lara stood side by side, just behind them stood Claws and 42.

They watched Vendax, the minnows hovered on their MIMs, waiting.

Vendax turned. He looked at the two tubes which held Jack's parents and he spoke to them.

"Well, John and Mary." Vendax spoke slowly. "It seems like I trained your son a little too well."

"Yes, Vendax you did," came a voice in reply.

Jack, Lara and Claws turned round in surprise. It was 42 who spoke.

"Yes, Jack," said 42 in his calm, steady voice. "It's me. It's Dad, Jack. It's been me all along."

"Dad?" gasped Jack.

Lara put her hand on a Jack's arm in support. He was shaking with surprise and shock.

"What? John?" asked Vendax, equally surprised.

"Yes. It is me. I am John Trainer." said 42. "Well, I am his mind anyway. My body is as you see it, in the med-tube there."

They all looked at the body of Jack's father suspended in the clear liquid of the tube, then back at 42. "Impossible!" Vendax hissed in shock.

"Really?" said 42 stepping forward towards Vendax. "Remember, it was I that designed the med-bots that you turned into kill-bots; it was I that designed the software. I set this robot up as a fail-safe, in case anything should happen to me. In case of an accident, I didn't know it would be you who would be the danger. You were a friend, Dax."

Vendax staggered slightly, then sat slowly down in his chair. 42 walked forward and stood in front of him.

"You are beginning to feel different aren't you?" said John Trainer through the body of 42. "The anger is fading isn't it?"

"What...?" whispered Vendax. " What have I done...?"

42 leaned forward, his robotic hand reached out and rested on Vendax's arm.

"I am sorry, Dax," said Jack's father. "It was my fault. The system wasn't ready, we weren't ready. When you had your accident we were distraught. Mary warned me, she told me to just let you go, she said that death was all part of life's natural cycle. I wouldn't listen. The only way to keep you alive was to use an untested med-bot, and an untested drug. It had side-effects which we did not forsee. It kept you conscious when you should have just slept, and the cocktail of chemicals overloaded your brain, it drove you mad, made you see everything as a threat."

Vendax stared at Jack, his shoulders slumped, the expression on his face although frozen, suddenly seemed sad.

"Everything was an enemy, I had to destroy, but how... how could I have thought that? How could I have done... those things...?" Vendax's voice broke with emotion.

"It was not you. It was this." answered Jack's father holding up the computer chip which he had taken from Vendax. "It reacted with the chemicals in your own body in a way we could never have expected. The fear and adrenaline in your system after your accident combined with this program, turned your survival instinct, your battle for life, and your – jealousy, into something uncontrollable.

It was not your fault, Dax. I am so sorry

for what you went through. I had no idea that you had feelings for Mary. We had no idea that you were awake, watching us, unable to sleep. It drove you out of your mind. We would never have done that to you intentionally.

"Mary," said Vendax. His body now slumped further into the chair as he reached out towards Jack's mother in the med-tube. "How could I have done this to her, I never meant to harm her... how could I have made her watch her own son suffer...?"

"She didn't, Dax," replied 42's calm voice. "The first thing I did was set her to sleep. She didn't see a thing. She didn't see Jack suffer. When I wake her up she will feel like she has only just gone to sleep."

"My eyes," said Vendax. His voice now weak. "Everything is fading, I can't see."

"Your robot suit is shutting down. Your senses are returning to your organic body, you can't live without the chip, Dax. You are fading. You are dying."

"Where is my body? My real body?" asked Vendax.

42 leaned forward and pressed a combination of switches on the side of the huge white robot. Vendax offered no resistance, all the fight was gone from him. There was a soft hum of internal motors and then a panel slid smoothly open in Vendax's chest.

Inside was a human head. Pale, motionless, eyes slightly open. The head sat in a clear liquid, it was connected to the inside of the robot with wires and softly flashing tubes.

The eyes in the head looked out, conscious, yet unmoving.

"I can see again... "came Vendax's faint voice. "I am me again...I am so sorry... I am so sorry..."

Then the voice faded to nothing and the lights in the white suit faded and went out.

Chapter 21

Rise of Vendax

"Dad...?" said Jack.

42 turned to face Jack, Lara and Claws.

"Yes, Jack, it is me," said 42.

"You were with us all this time?" asked Jack. "Why didn't you tell us?"

"I didn't know if you would believe me," replied 42, "and if you did, what if I had been killed again? I didn't want you to lose me twice. I didn't want you to worry about me; I just wanted to be there for you."

"I have so many questions - what happened?" asked Jack.

"Dax was my friend," said 42. "We were scientists at this research station. We were working on a medical robot which would be a host to the mind of people who were badly injured or paralysed; it was supposed to give a body to those whose bodies were damaged beyond repair, it was supposed to be a new life for those who had lost everything. We made breakthrough after breakthrough. We were young and ambitious; we thought we would change the world, we thought our names would go down in history.

Then the shuttle-craft in which Dax was flying was caught in a meteor storm, he nearly made it back, but crashed. We rushed to save him, but his body was hopelessly wrecked. I kept him alive in a med-tube and decided to keep him there until I had completed my research, until a prototype med-bot was built. It took longer than we thought; we had no idea that he was conscious, or of the effect the psychotropic drugs we gave him would have.

I knew that if anything happened to me then all my research would be lost, as a precaution I decided to set up a link from my mind to this robot in case something should happen to me. I wanted Mary to do the same, but she refused.

Finally the med-bot prototype was ready for Dax. We connected what remained of him physically; just his head, to the white robot, then linked his mind to the machine.

He came to life and immediately attacked us. We managed to escape and went to a remote planet and built a simple life together. We thought we were hidden, we thought we were safe, but Dax, now the white robot 'Vendax' tracked us down. He captured us and imprisoned us in these med-tubes.

Unknown to him, my mind transferred immediately to this robot. I was able to re-set your mother's tube so that she would be asleep, held in stasis. I stayed here right under his nose, trying to work out a plan, waiting for a moment to make my move. I knew I had to find you, but I didn't know where to look, I didn't want to leave your mother. Years went by until finally I had news of you.

I heard that Vendax planned to attack and destroy Truno Abbey. At last I knew where to look, I followed him there, but arrived too late. I saw you in the Silver FOX being chased by terror-naughts; I took a chance and jumped for your ship, I nearly didn't make it. I didn't think you would trust me. I had heard Vendax talk about the Omicron; I heard him say that you would be looking for all its crystal jewels - I didn't know it was a trick. I thought that together we could destroy Vendax and free Mary.

"And you did," said Lara.

"Yes, we did," said Jack. "I can't believe its been you all along."

Jack put his hand on 42's metal arm.

"Now it is time to set her free," said Jack's father through 42.

"Now it's time to set you free too," replied Jack. "- Now it's time to set them all free."

They looked about them at the millions of bodies; each one alive, each one a person to be returned home.

Suddenly they were all struck by the thought of all those people being re-united with their loved-ones again; fathers, mothers, sisters, brothers, husbands and wives, sons and daughters, all being able to see their families again. A wave of happiness swept over them.

"We have quite a job to do," said Jack. "We have to get them all home."

"All in good time!" said 42 to Jack. "Right now, what I want to know is, what in the galaxy are you playing at?"

Jack was taken aback.

"What do you mean?" he asked.

"For goodness sake! When are you going to tell this beautiful girl that you love her?" With that he pointed to Lara.

Lara blushed, her cheeks turning a soft purple.

Jack looked at Lara, he reached out and took her hands.

"I do love you, Lara," said Jack.

"I love you too," answered Lara.

Their lips met.

42 looked at Claws.

"Well, thank goodness for that - about time too!"

Claws laughed. Minnow jumped up onto Jack's shoulder.

"Minnow! Minnow!" he chirped triumphantly.

All the Minnow-kind, sitting on their bleeping MIMs answered him in chorus.

"Minnow, Minnow, Minnow!"

Chapter 22

A Home on Duatha

It is a beautiful day. The sun is shining, birds singing. It is summer on Duatha, the grass is green and there are flowers everywhere.

"Here they come!" says Jack.

Lara appears from their house set in the hill-side. In her arms is their baby. She smiles.

A short distance away is the Silver FOX; next to it three other ships are coming in to land.

From out of the first ship walks Jack's mum and dad: John and Mary

Trainer, well and happy, smiling and waving. They embrace Jack and Lara in happy greeting, smiling at the new-born baby.

The second ship is the Wave Star, from inside it appear Captain Flash and Kendra, arm-in-arm.

Flash looks at Kendra adoringly.

"You are so beautiful!" he says gazing wistfully into her eyes.

"Oh shoosh! I bet you say that to all the girls!" She kisses him and laughs, shaking her long blonde hair in the breeze.

"Come on, Mum and Dad!" laughs Flash, looking behind him into the ship. We don't want you old people keeping us waiting!"

Flash's father and mother appear, from the ship behind them. They are also safe and well. Flash's father with mock annoyance slaps Flash's shoulder.

"Oi!" he says, "less of the 'old'!"

As Flash and his family walk towards Jack and Lara to also offer their congratulations at their new baby, from the other ship appears Claws.

"Aarggghclaaaw!" cries Claws raising high in the air a large bottle of wine, his purple fur rippling in the breeze, his mouth open in a wide grin.

Then suddenly, at top speed out of the ship's hatchway, behind Claws speeds Minnow, riding as usual his robot friend MIM.

Everyone laughs as the pair zoom around them in joyous circles, MIM uttering high-pitched bleeps and Minnow on its back, his long, pink arm raised in the air, eyes closed, fluffy white fur flowing behind him singing a long happy cry -

"Minnoooooooow!"

"Jack and Lara," says Jack's Dad.

"I have a present for you. You can come out now!" He calls towards his ship.

There are slow heavy footsteps, and then out of the ship appears Centurion 42.

"42?" asks Jack in surprise.

"It's the same robot, it took some time, but I worked out how to let him operate independently. I have programmed him to remember your adventures; I thought you might like a little help around the farm and he can also translate the cat's language for you!" smiles Jack's dad.

"Hello sir," says 42 in his calm metallic voice. "I see you are celebrating. May I suggest some refreshments?"

They all laugh.

"That would be perfect, 42, thank you," said Jack. "It wouldn't be the same without you."

Their glasses full; Jack raises his in toast.

"Here is to all of us! To family! To friends ... of every shape and size!

 - We have voyaged all over the galaxy, but in the end - there's no place like home."

Then all the family and friends gather round Jack and Lara, smiling at their new pale-blue baby; happy in the knowledge that Vendax was gone, and that this child would grow up always being safe, loved and free.

Little did they know, that in fact things would work out rather differently - but that, is another story.....

Galaxy Voyage Part 1:

The Dragons of Doom

Fast-paced, high-speed, non-stop, laser-blasting, action and adventure!

Orphans Jack and Lara lose everything when evil Lord Vendax and his robot armies destroy their home. Fleeing on board their spaceship - the Silver FOX, they begin a perilous voyage across the galaxy in search of the crystals which can activate a secret weapon and destroy Vendax.

Helped by the mysterious robot - Centurion 42, a purple, four armed cat named Claws, and Minnow - a chattering, white ball of fluff, Jack and Lara battle against killer-robots, flesh-eating plants, giant spiders and the dragons of Doom themselves in their quest to restore justice to the galaxy.

Galaxy Voyage Part 2:

The Sandvipers of Zaak

Jack, Lara, 42, Claws and Minnow continue their heroic voyage across the galaxy in this next exciting installment of the Galaxy Voyage trilogy.

The crew of the Silver FOX are whisked onwards on their dangerous journey - first to the ice planet of Sowan, where in the frozen wastelands, they face a host of monstrous snow-beasts; then to the desert planet of Zaak, where with new found friends, they battle gigantic scorpions and killer snakes in search of the next crystal jewels for the Omicron.

With Vendax and his robot armies in relentless pursuit, this action packed sequel propels the companions from one danger to another in their continuing quest across the stars.

About the author

L.D.P. Stead

Laurence Stead is a primary school teacher and father of two, who lives in Brighton, England.

His interests include: movies, playing and recording music, photography and video, collecting retro toys, walking in the countryside, art and design, history and science.

Galaxy Voyage is his debut as a children's fiction writer and is a celebration of his life-long enjoyment of science fiction, fantasy and adventure stories.

www.galaxy-voyage.co.uk

Printed in Great Britain
by Amazon